# DANGEROUS ENCOUNTER

After Kate Summers witnesses a violent stabbing, she finds herself running for her life. Along with her two children, she moves to a small Cornish town, where they live quietly and anonymously as they try to start afresh. Then Kate encounters the handsome Ross St. Clair, and her life begins to change again. When she senses danger once more, she knows she has to keep herself and her children safe from harm. But how?

SUSAN UDY

# DANGEROUS ENCOUNTER

*Complete and Unabridged*

**LINFORD**
*Leicester*

First published in Great Britain

First Linford Edition
published 2017

A catalogue record for this book is available
from the British Library.

ISBN 978–1–4448–3295–2

Published by
F. A. Thorpe (Publishing)
Anstey, Leicestershire

Set by Words & Graphics Ltd.
Anstey, Leicestershire
Printed and bound in Great Britain by
T. J. International Ltd., Padstow, Cornwall

This book is printed on acid-free paper

# 1

Shaken to her core, Kate Summers stared at the tall, powerfully built man who'd just walked into the room.

It was him. The man who'd followed her home on that March evening just a few weeks ago. The man who'd stood in the dark on the opposite side of the road to her house. The man who'd raised his arm and pointed two fingers at her, miming the aiming of a gun, before mouthing 'Pow'. The man she'd seen commit murder only moments before. Robert Wilmot, or Rob the Knife as he was known in the criminal underworld.

But how could he possibly be here in Cornwall? He was in prison awaiting trial, wasn't he? He must be. She'd have been informed if he'd been released or had escaped, surely? Yet here was this man who looked exactly like him. The same build, the same height — the same colour hair, even — though it had been dark at the time, so she couldn't be a hundred percent sure about that. Was it possible he had been released and had managed to trace her whereabouts? Her heart pounded, and her stomach convulsed with panic.

She forced herself to calm down, and looked again. Gradually, as her breathing slowed, she came to the conclusion that this wasn't the same man. She could be forgiven, however, for having initially thought he was, because the similarity to the person she'd indentified from police mug shots was quite remarkable.

But as she watched him, she realised — too late — that he'd been fully aware of her scrutiny. His well-shaped mouth curved into a smile as he returned her stare; it was a very self-assured smile, to the point of smugness actually, as if he considered such intense interest fully justified.

Kate's lips tightened. Not only was he manifestly self-satisfied, he was the picture of arrogance as well. It showed in the way he was standing; the way he held his head high — loftily high, in fact — making it more than evident that he considered himself vastly superior to everyone else in the room. She'd always disliked men like that, and she'd known one or two in her time. They invariably treated women badly, herself being one of them. One in particular, she recalled. She'd been eighteen and highly impressionable; Sean Brady had been his name. He'd been tall, with piercing blue eyes, and he'd been the image of Pierce Brosnan. Predictably, she'd fallen head over heels in love. But unbeknownst to her, he'd been seeing several other girls at the same time he'd been dating her. It had been a friend who'd finally taken pity on her and told her, and she'd never forgotten the humiliation of it — the whispering and giggling among girls she'd considered her friends; the sly, hurtful digs about her foolish naivety. In the wake of that, she'd sworn to steer well clear of overly good-looking, arrogant men. So when, not long afterwards, she'd met Simon, who had been modestly good-looking as well as kind and thoughtful, she'd quickly fallen in love. Genuinely in love. They'd married eighteen months later and had their first child eighteen months after that.

Now, as she and the handsome stranger stared at each other, each seemingly unwilling to be the first to look away, Kate's friend Morwenna broke in to say, 'Kate, I'd like you to meet a very good friend of mine and Brett's: Ross St. Clair.'

Kate regarded Morwenna with amusement. Ross St. Clair? Such a pretentious name. Of course someone like this man, patently self-satisfied and utterly confident, would answer to such a surname.

She returned her gaze to his face. A pair of amber eyes met hers as heavy lids belatedly shuttered his thoughts. Nonetheless, his smile broadened into one of unabashed appreciation as he let his narrowed gaze roam over her features, from her shoulder-length Titian-coloured hair to her hazel eyes, green in some lights, and her high cheekbones and full, rose-pink lips.

'Ross,' Morwenna went on, sublimely unaware of the interplay between her two guests, 'meet Kate Summers, a relatively recent arrival in Bodruggan.' She swung back to her friend. 'Ross only returned from an extended business trip to Australia a couple of weeks ago.'

'Oh?' Kate tersely responded. 'How long were you there for?' she asked, whilst thinking to herself what a pity it was he hadn't stayed there.

'A couple of months, give or take a week or so. And I have to say, it's good to be back.' His eyes danced at her. 'And even better to discover a new and very attractive face to look at. I love the hair, by the way,' he went on. 'Presumably, it indicates a temper.'

She said nothing. She certainly wasn't going to admit that at times, if she was sufficiently provoked, it most certainly did. She wouldn't allow him the gratification of knowing he'd presumed correctly. But then, just as if he'd read her thoughts, he gave a soft snort of what sounded like mirth. She glared at him, mutely daring him to say anything else.

Fortunately, at that point he turned his attention to Morwenna, who was saying, 'Of course, Ross, you know everyone else here.' She indicated the other guests, who had remained totally silent throughout this exchange.

Kate also knew them, if only by sight. They'd been introduced as Sally and David Feeley, Barbara and Dennis Bailey, and Margaret — better known as Mags — and her husband Paul Wheeler. This was, however, the first time that Kate had had the chance to do more than smile and say hello. They were all people who had lived in the town for many years, as had Morwenna and Brett.

Morwenna grinned saucily at Kate, and Kate suddenly realised she'd been specifically invited as a partner for Ross St. Clair. Sadly, Morwenna was a stickler for doing the right thing, and the right thing in this case was to invite an even number of guests to dinner. Well, Kate silently scoffed, if she thought for a minute that

Kate and Ross St.-bloody-Clair would hit it off, she was miles wide of the mark. Because as she'd already decided, he was exactly the sort of man she'd gone to great lengths always to avoid. Too good-looking by half; too sure of himself and his own worth. Too everything, really. She frowned then. Surely a man like him would have his own partner to bring, or even a wife? He looked to be in his late thirties. She couldn't imagine he'd need to be set up with what was little better than a blind date.

Kate had met Morwenna Lucas within days of her arrival in town six weeks ago. Morwenna worked a couple of mornings a week in the local museum. Kate had ventured in, hoping to discover something of the history of the town, about which she knew absolutely nothing. They'd started chatting, and within minutes it had felt as if they'd always been friends. Although Morwenna was forty-two — almost forty-three, she frequently bemoaned — to Kate's thirty-one, they'd got along well enough to subsequently meet up a couple of times afterward for an early supper at one of the local pubs, The Ship. Morwenna's sixteen-year-old daughter, Pattie, babysat for Kate's two young children, Ellie and Matt, ten and eight years old respectively.

It was with considerable relief that Kate turned in response to Mags's interruption. 'So, how are you liking our little town, Kate? We pride ourselves on being visitor-friendly.'

Kate couldn't help but be a little stung at the implication that she was just a visitor. However, she kept her feelings to herself — Mags clearly didn't know she was here to stay. 'I love it, thank you, Mags.'

'How long are you here for? I believe you're staying at Honeysuckle Cottage? It's been empty for quite a while, so it's good to have someone in residence, if only for a short time.'

'Yes, that's right, and I plan to stay.'

'Oh?' Mags raised an eyebrow. In censure? Kate wondered. Or was she being unnecessarily sensitive? Yet, it certainly looked that way. Even the other woman's tone was a sharp one. It suggested she resented any newcomers to the town. 'I'd heard it was just a summer let.'

'No.' Kate gradually had become aware that Ross St. Clair was listening to the exchange. So not only was he a lech, he was nosey to boot. 'We're here for the duration.'

'We?' Mags again raised an eyebrow, the other one this time. Again, it seemed to signal disapproval.

Despite Kate's growing irritation, she stared at it, almost mesmerised. She'd never been able to do that. On the couple of occasions she'd tried — in front of a mirror, luckily — she hadn't been able to stop both eyebrows going up, bestowing an astonished and faintly ridiculous look. So she'd given up on that, and instead, when she wanted to indicate displeasure or any other similar emotion, she simply frowned. Much less effort, in her opinion.

'Yes,' Kate told her. She might as well get the facts out now, the true facts, before the local gossip machine rumbled into action. 'My children and I.'

'How many children do you have?'

'Two. Ellie and Matt. They're both attending the local school.'

'Really?' This time both eyebrows shot up. And now Kate definitely recognised disapproval. Was everyone going to be this critical of her family's arrival in town? Would everybody be so tribal? She hoped not, but it did make her question whether she'd done the right thing in coming to this small town, where she was beginning to suspect everyone knew everyone else's business and, evidently, had an opinion about it. An opinion they had no hesitation in expressing, whether by gesture or word.

'A little late, isn't it?' Mags went on. 'They'll be breaking up for the summer in just over a couple of months.'

'Well, they actually started just after Easter, so they'll have been there a bit longer than a couple of months. I thought it best to get them settled in and ready to return after the long holiday in September. The headmistress agreed with me.'

'How old are they?'

This was fast turning into something of an inquisition, Kate irritably decided. Nevertheless, she replied, 'Ten and eight.'

'And where have you come from?'

'The midlands.'

'I see. And what made you decide to come here? I assume it's just you and your children.'

'Yes, it is. My husband died ... ' Her voice faltered, as it always did when she spoke about Simon. ' ... a year ago in a car accident. I thought a change of scene would help the children as well as myself. Help us to put it behind us. Not that we'll ever forget him. But we have to move on.'

Ross was taking all of this in. Kate glanced sideways at him; her expression, she guessed, one of vexation. Why couldn't he mind his own business? But surprisingly, it was compassion that she saw dawning in his eyes. Maybe he did have a softer side, after all.

'Well,' Mags said, 'you've certainly got yourself a change of scene, Cornwall instead of the midlands. The two places couldn't be more different. And I'm very sorry that you and your children have had to suffer such a terrible tragedy.' This time there was no hint of any sort of disapproval. It had been replaced by sympathy. 'So tell me, are the children liking it here? It must be a tremendous upheaval for them both.'

At this juncture, Kate noticed she had become the focus of everyone's attention; they were all listening intently to what she was saying. 'Ellie's doing okay, but Matt ... ' For the second time, her voice faltered and broke. 'He's not doing as well. He was close to his father and he still misses him badly.'

'Well ...' This was Ross speaking. Kate swivelled to look at him. ' ... let me say you're very welcome here, and if there's anything I or anyone else can do, please just ask. For my part, I'd be very willing to help out with anything you need.'

For the second time, Kate spotted compassion in those amber eyes, making her question whether she'd been too hasty in her initial judgement of him. 'Thank you,' she replied. 'I appreciate that. Do you live in Bodruggan?'

Mags had moved away, thankfully. Up until the final moment or two, Kate had sensed unmistakable criticism in the tone of the other woman's remarks and questions, and she didn't think it was just her imagination, which she admitted was prone to run riot at times. Anyway, imagined or not, the other woman's responses to her remarks had made her feel more than a tad unwelcome. Maybe the local people resented new arrivals from another part of the country. Or, maybe, she belatedly reflected, the other woman's attitude had more to do with the manner in which her husband, Paul, had been showing more than a casual interest in Kate and her replies. In fact, just like Ross St. Clair's, his gaze had roved all over her, his expression one of undisguised admiration — lust, even — as he watched her, which he'd been doing with increasing frequency.

'I do live here,' Ross said. 'Well, a few

miles outside, actually, towards Truro. Bodruggan House. Do you know it?'

'No, I don't.'

'You'll have to come and visit then. Meet my daughter, Cleo.'

'And your wife? She's not with you this evening?'

'My wife and I divorced four years ago. Cleo refused to go and live with her mother, who's remarried and now lives in a Scottish castle in the Highlands, complete with its own loch. But Cleo was unimpressed by any of it.' His lips quirked with amusement as his eyes glittered. 'She declared there was no way she was going to live in the wilds of Scotland, out in the sticks as she described it. She'd rather die, she then melodramatically announced.'

Kate grinned at him and watched as his smile vanished and his face paled; he looked as if someone or something had struck him a hard blow. 'Are you okay?' she asked.

'I'm fine,' he assured her, somewhat shakily.

'So how old is she?'

But he had swiftly regained his former composure, making Kate wonder whether she'd imagined his stunned look, and replied with his former self-assurance. 'Fourteen, going on twenty-four.'

Kate grimaced then. 'Oh dear, I can see you might have a few problems.'

'A few?' he scoffed. 'There's a new one every day.'

'Could it be that she's missing her mother more than you realise?'

'It's possible.' He gave a rueful smile. 'Other than my housekeeper, Beth Elliot, she doesn't get much adult female input. Beth's very good with her, though.'

Again, Kate was surprised. In the absence of a wife, she would have expected him to have a girlfriend, or a mistress, somewhere in the background, even if he didn't bring her to occasions like this dinner party. 'So there's no second Mrs St. Clair on the scene?' She darted a glance round the room, as if searching for a possible candidate.

'No. Why? Are you applying for the position?' Amusement again made its appearance in the form of several minute gold glints in his eyes.

Kate stiffened. What the hell had possessed her, to ask such a personal question? She eyed her almost-empty wine glass in disgust. She'd never been able to handle much more than a glassful over an entire evening, and she usually stuck to that. But now here she was, lacking even a modicum of common sense, having downed the lot in a mere half an hour. All because she'd known she'd be meeting several new people and had felt the need of a boost to her confidence. Mind you, if she'd had any idea that someone like Ross St. Clair would be here, she'd have turned down Morwenna's invitation. Again, without thinking, she blurted, 'Certainly not.'

He didn't answer straight away. But then: 'That unpleasant a prospect, is it?' His voice was level and almost toneless, but the look in his eyes was a piercing one. So piercing, in fact, that Kate had no trouble believing he was drilling his way through her skull and reading every one of her thoughts.

As a consequence, her words were terse and to the point. 'I can't comment. I don't know you.'

'Well, maybe you should. We're both adults ... single. What's to stop us getting together, getting to know each other?'

'Maybe the fact that we've only just met,' she bit back.

'Why should that be a hindrance? Everyone has to meet for the first time at some point. Come out with me for a meal tomorrow evening. I don't bite, honest.'

The look in his eyes now was a distinctly challenging one. And that last remark — huh! She was sure he would bite, given the opportunity. 'No, thank you.' No way was she going out for anything with him. She wouldn't trust him as far as she could throw him. It would be her and Sean Brady all over again. He had the same characteristics that Sean had possessed — good looks, too much self-confidence. The absolute certainty that women would fall over themselves to go out with him.

'Why not?' he asked, before adding in

17

an undertone, 'Frightened?'

Infuriated by the knowing glint in his amber eyes, she gave a scornful snort. 'Of you? Why would I be?'

He shrugged, drawing her gaze to the breadth of his shoulders beneath his immaculately tailored coffee-coloured jacket. 'You tell me.'

Deliberately she let her gaze roam over him now, just as he'd done with her, taking in his moderately long toffee-coloured hair, his unusual eyes, his Grecian nose and well-shaped mouth, his sculpted cheekbones and chiselled jawline. Sadly, though, her boldness almost at once rebounded on her, because the glints reappeared in his eyes.

He throatily murmured, 'Like what you see?'

She could tell from the way his mouth curled up at the corners that he guessed she did. However, she wasn't about to admit as much. In fact, given the choice between death and that sort of admission, she'd opt for death any day. 'I have no feelings either way,' she coolly told him.

'Liar,' he murmured.

'I don't lie,' she sharply told him. Even though he was absolutely right.

'What, never? Not even a white one?'

'Not if I can help it.' Which was yet another lie, albeit a very small one. Would he pick up on that too? She wouldn't be surprised. This man was turning into an infuriating enigma, and that was simply intensifying her feelings of unease.

But he must have decided to let that one pass, because all he said was, 'Okay. Well, I'd like to see you again.'

*Tough*, was her silent response to that. *You're not going to. At least, not on a date.* All she said, however, was, 'That's impossible.'

'Why's that? Do you turn into a pumpkin if you're out at night?'

'Hardly,' she scoffed. 'I'm here now.'

'So you are.' He fell silent for a moment, contenting himself with simply observing her from beneath heavy eyelids. 'So why won't you come out with me?'

'I have two young children.'

'I know. You must have someone who

can babysit for you? Who's doing it this evening?'

'Pattie will come round for you, Kate.' It was Morwenna. She'd clearly been eavesdropping on their conversation, or at least part of it. But that was Morwenna — nosey, though she described it as a perfectly natural interest in others. 'The children know her.'

Kate bit at her bottom lip. Now what? 'No, really. Thank you, Morwenna, but no.' And she glared meaningfully at her friend.

Morwenna picked up on the look straight away. 'Okay.' And she too drifted away.

But Ross wasn't going to allow Kate to wriggle out of things a second time. 'So, there we are. All arranged.'

'No. Sorry, but no. I don't date.'

'Okay, so we won't call it a date. We'll call it a social engagement.'

Couldn't the wretched man take no for an answer? 'The answer's still no, I'm afraid — whatever you choose to call it.'

Heavy lids lowered over gleaming eyes

as he softly said, 'Chicken.'

Once again she stiffened. What a detestable man. Despite her reservations of a moment ago, she decided that her first judgement of him had clearly been the correct one. He was so arrogant that he couldn't believe a woman wouldn't leap at the chance to go out with him. Well, he'd soon learn she was a woman of her word, and that when she said no, she flippin' well meant no.

Pretending she hadn't heard him, she turned to Sally Feeley and began to chat to her. It didn't help. Ross's gaze burned into the back of her, and when he leant forward and murmured into her ear, 'I always get my way in the end — it's simply a matter of time,' she was tempted to use some rather objectionable language. She didn't, of course. Mainly because she didn't want him to know how deeply he was affecting her. She had no desire to add to his overbearing — no, that word didn't even begin to describe it anywhere near accurately enough — his *monumental* self-confidence. Instead, she began to talk with great animation to a startled Sally.

'Tell me about your family, Sally,' she said. But before Sally could do so, Morwenna called out that dinner was ready, and they all migrated into the dining room.

To Kate's enormous relief, Morwenna directed Ross to the other end of the table, on the same side as Kate but, thankfully, with Mags and Dennis between them. Morwenna must have realised things weren't destined to proceed smoothly between the two of them, and had decided to abandon her attempt at matchmaking. Anyway, whatever her friend's reasons, her actions ensured Kate didn't have to either look at or speak to Ross St. Clair.

The drawback to that, however, was the sight of Paul sitting almost opposite her, which meant that once again she found herself the object of his smouldering gaze for almost the entire meal. Lord knew what Mags must have thought, though the fact that the other woman barely addressed a word to Kate was a fairly reliable indication that she wasn't happy. No wonder she'd sounded resentful earlier on. It hadn't been because she disliked Kate; after all, she didn't know her. No. She'd clearly noticed her husband's frequent and admiring glances Kate's way.

# 2

All in all, Kate was heartily relieved when eleven thirty finally arrived and she could justifiably leave. However, just as she was about to slip her arms into her jacket, Ross strode over and bluntly asked, 'How did you get here?'

She stared at him, taken aback by the question. 'I walked.'

'Well, you can't walk back; it's too late. I'll take you.'

She drew a deep breath in a vain attempt to ease the surge of indignation his high-handed declaration had provoked. But all that did was encourage his gaze to drop to her noticeably swelling breasts. Hoping to end the display she'd so heedlessly provided, she slowly released her breath again. It made not one iota of difference. His gaze continued to linger upon her, lazily moving down to take in the slender waist and gently curving hips, just as it had done when they'd been first introduced. Was there no stopping the wretched man? Not only was he disgustingly lecherous, but he also assumed he had the right to tell her what she could and couldn't do. He needed to be put right on the latter, at least, and be told in no uncertain terms that she was someone who made her own decisions.

'I don't need anyone to escort me home,' she said, 'and certainly not someone I've only just met and know nothing about. I only live a few moments' walk away, so I'll be perfectly safe.' Her tone was scornful and curt, unequivocally illustrating her dislike of his manner and words, but she didn't care. She wasn't usually this outspoken, but he needed to understand that she was accountable to no one, and certainly not to him, a complete stranger. 'This is Bodruggan after all, not some big city,' she added, at the same time allowing herself to give what she hoped was a withering smile.

To her frustration, however, that too was wasted on him. In fact, she suspected he didn't even notice, due to the fact that he was in no hurry to lift his gaze from the curves still on show. When he finally did so, he proceeded to regard her flushed cheeks and blazing eyes with what looked like complete indifference to her show of outrage. Again, she was forced to take a deep breath as she struggled for calm. However, this time he didn't as much as glance at the display in front of him, which paradoxically only intensified her exasperation with him.

'As you wish,' he drawled. 'So who's babysitting this evening?'

Good grief, he was like a terrier with a bone. Why the hell couldn't he let the matter drop? 'A local woman I know.'

'She does that often for you, does she?'

Too late, she heard the snapping of the trap he'd sneakily set. 'No, she doesn't. This is the first time.'

'Well, I'm sure she'll agree to do it a second time. So, once again, will you come out with me?'

'And I'll say — again, no.'

'Why the hell not?'

She glimpsed the first indication of a temper. Until then, he'd remained maddeningly cool and composed. 'Because I don't want to. I've got no intention of becoming involved with a man, any man. My children are all I care about at the moment. They've had enough upset in their lives without me adding more.'

He shrugged, but this time unquestioningly accepted her refusal. 'Okay. Well, as I mentioned earlier, you know where I am if you need me.'

'Oh, I doubt that will happen,' she snapped.

He didn't respond, but simply stared at her, his eyes dark and stormy, his mouth a tightly compressed line as a muscle flexed in his granite jaw. 'I'll just say goodnight then. I wish you well. I'll probably see you around. I get out and about quite a bit.'

'I'm sure you do,' she muttered.

Again, he declined to answer that gibe and instead swung and strode away, his expression an impenetrable one.

Kate watched him go and for the first time felt a small pang of regret. But how could she possibly get involved with any man, considering her current situation? She couldn't tell him the truth. She couldn't tell anyone — not even Morwenna, no matter how much she longed to. Not for the first time, she acknowledged how completely alone she was, despite the friends she was making; and a sensation of unutterable desolation and despair engulfed her.

* * *

If only she hadn't gone out that fateful evening, Kate reflected as she recalled the past events that had led to her current situation here in Cornwall. But she had, and now she had to live with the consequences.

It had been a little after ten o'clock, and she'd been walking home alone, having met a couple of friends for a drink. Her mother had been babysitting, so she hadn't wanted to be late.

She'd been a fifteen-minute walk from home in a suburb of Birmingham. She'd felt no fear about being alone; the area was a respectable one and had always been considered safe. Street lights and an occasional tree lined the pavement at fairly regular intervals. But on that particular evening, a couple of the lights hadn't been working. Even then, she hadn't felt nervous — until, in the darkness beneath one of these two, she'd spotted a couple of men. At first she'd believed they were simply horsing around, pushing at each other and talking in loud voices. It hadn't been until she heard one of them shouting, 'Leave me alone, you bastard,' and she saw the glint of what she thought was the blade of a knife, that she realised it was far more serious than just two men arguing.

She'd stopped walking and crept beneath the low-hanging branches of the nearby tree. What she witnessed then made her give a low moan and start to tremble. She wrapped her arms tightly about her middle, as if that would offer her some form of protection, and then gasped again as what was definitely the blade of a knife flashed several times, as one man stabbed the other over and over, grimly saying, 'This is what you get for moving onto my turf, for trying to take my business.' The man under attack had fallen and now lay motionless. He made no sound, and Kate thought she could see blood gradually creeping across the pavement.

The attacker then straightened up and glanced around, up and down the street, before, to Kate's horror, looking across the road, straight at her. She shrank back into the shadows, making herself as small as she possibly could, but it was no good. He stared directly at her. He'd seen her.

Knowing there was no other option open to her, she bolted from the shadows and began to run. Thankfully, she was wearing trainers and jeans, so she was able to swiftly pick up her pace. She'd been a champion sprinter at school, invariably winning all her races. The ability stood her in good stead now; that and the flood of adrenaline that swamped her, lengthening her stride and increasing her pace. She didn't look back, not even when she heard the sound of heavy footsteps gaining on her. She literally ran for her life. She knew beyond any shadow of a doubt that if he caught her, he'd kill her. He'd have to, and her children would be orphans …

Her breath was erupting in huge gasps. She felt herself begin to tire, her legs aching and weakening; but she could see her house just ahead. If she could only keep going …

He was getting closer. She could feel him, almost; feel his breath on the back of her neck. She made one final, superhuman effort, and suddenly she was racing towards her front door. Frantic by this time to get off the street, she hammered on it, at the same time pressing her finger hard on the doorbell. She hadn't bothered taking a key with her.

'Mum!' she screamed. 'Open the door!'

The hall light came on and the door was flung open. She threw herself inside, slamming it closed behind her and engaging the deadlock, just in case.

Her mother looked startled and more than a little frightened. 'What's the matter? What's wrong?'

'I-I ... ' Kate bent double as she struggled to get her breath and speak. Even so, her words were garbled, almost incoherent, as they cascaded from her lips. 'I-I think I s-saw someone murdered. I-I witnessed a stabbing. He-he saw me, he followed me.' She ran into the sitting room and to the window that overlooked the road. 'He knows where I live.' And sure enough, when she tweaked the curtain a fraction to one side, he was out there, standing on the opposite pavement, staring straight back at her.

All of a sudden he raised an arm, pointed two fingers at her as if he were aiming a gun, and mouthed a silent 'Pow'.

Kate dropped the curtain and sprang backwards, almost knocking her ashen-faced mother over. 'What shall I do?' she sobbed. 'He's out there. He'll kill me, too.'

But amazingly her mother sounded perfectly calm, despite what Kate had

32

just told her. 'You call the police, right now. That's what you do. Here.' She reached for the cordless phone that was on a nearby table before thrusting it into Kate's trembling hand.

And that was the start of it all.

Once Kate had reported that she thought she'd seen someone murdered in Manor Road, and the murderer was standing outside of her house, the police quickly arrived; by which time, of course, the killer had gone. She again related exactly what she'd seen to the two plainclothes officers and said that he had followed her home, his subsequent actions looking to her like a serious threat.

They then informed her that two of their fellow officers had immediately gone to the crime scene and reported back that the man was indeed dead. 'Did you get a good look at the perpetrator?' they asked.

'Yes, but it was dark.'

'Okay. Well, we need you to come to the station in the morning and take a look at some mug shots of known criminals. Till then, we'll arrange for a car outside, and two officers will keep watch on the house overnight.'

Once they'd gone, and Kate checked that there was indeed a car parked outside, Grace, her mother, got ready to return home. 'Are you sure you don't want me to stay?' she offered one last time. 'I can, easily.'

Kate's father had died ten years earlier, the result of a brain tumour, so Grace had no one to rush home to. But Kate refused to place her mother in danger by having her stay, so she insisted she go. She'd come by car, which she'd had to park a little way away, so the killer wouldn't have seen it or its number plate and thus been able to trace her address, which meant she wasn't in any danger from him. At least, Kate hoped not.

After a sleepless night, she'd gone to the police station, where she identified the man she'd seen.

'Are you positive?' one of the officers asked.

'Ninety, ninety-five percent, yes. But as I told you last night, it was very dark, as the street light was out, so his features weren't terribly clear. The overall impression I had was of someone who looked just like him.' And she pointed to the head and shoulders photo. It was of a good-looking man with a head of dark blond hair and pale eyes. He didn't resemble, in any way, her notion of a killer.

'Okay. Good. That's Robert Wilmot, a man well-known to us.'

She'd shuddered with horror as she wondered what he'd do to her if he ever got hold of her; if he returned to the house to find her. Her instincts told her he'd kill her. He'd have nothing to lose, after all. He'd already killed once.

'He's known as Rob the knife, so that fits with what you told us,' the DI explained. 'The trouble is,' he added, regarding Kate anxiously, 'he's a leading member of a particularly ruthless gang. They're into all sorts: protection rackets; theft — mainly cars at the high end of the spectrum, which they sell on the European market; drugs; murder, as you've seen for yourself. We've never been able to prove anything against any of them. Never been able to gather enough evidence to convict. People won't speak out, not even the ones they've hurt or stolen from. Too scared of reprisals. I'm hoping you'll be different. Because I'm afraid to say they'll be gunning for you, as you actually saw him commit murder. So I'm going to put something to you in a moment.' He paused briefly. 'A couple of officers will go and pick him up immediately. We know where he'll be, where he always is. He's really not very bright. Which means he'll be soon be safely behind bars — where, as you've definitely identified him, he'll stay until he comes to trial. If you'll agree to give evidence as an eye witness against him in court, and help us to convict him this time and put him away, we'll immediately place you in our witness protection scheme.'

*Oh my God* was Kate's first thought. She'd heard of this. Did she really want it? She'd seen a programme once on television about it. You virtually disappeared, leaving everyone behind — your family, your friends. 'What about my children?'

'They'll go with you. If you agree, we'll take you all to a hotel this afternoon where you'll be given new identities, new life histories, and then we'll transport you to a safe house where you'll stay, at least until after the court case. We'd really recommend you do this. If you don't, we can't answer for your or your children's safety. Any member of the gang would be prepared to kill you — in revenge, if nothing else — so even though Robert Wilmot will be in police custody prior to trial, well ... ' He shrugged. He didn't need to put it into words. Kate knew what he meant. Someone could — probably would — still try to kill her, even if Robert Wilmot was behind bars.

'O-okay.' What choice did she have? 'What about my mother? My sister? Lizzie still lives with my mother, for most of the time. They're the only family I have.'

'They'll be safe. He won't know them or where they are; neither will any of his gang. We'll keep an eye on them, in any case, for a while.'

'But will I be able to contact them or see them?'

''Fraid not. Once you've gone, there has to be no further contact with anyone you know. Not if you want to all be fully protected.'

Kate felt the sting of tears. The very notion was unimaginable. To not see her mother, her sister, her friends ... But again, what choice did she have, realistically? None.

'Okay, I'll do it.' She couldn't endanger her children, not even to keep in touch with her family.

'Right. You go home and pack bags. We'll collect you at midday, then go and get the children out of school.'

'What about all our other things?'

'You'll have to leave them behind, I'm afraid.'

'But what about the house?' Simon's insurance on his death had paid the mortgage off, but it would be left empty, uncared for. She could even lose it.

And what then? There'd be nothing to return to — in the event that she ever did return.

'That'll all be taken care of,' one of the officers assured her. 'You just worry about yourself and the kids. And you need to leave ASAP.'

So that was what happened. But she did take the time to ring her mother and tell her what was happening.

'Oh no!' Grace had cried. 'And the children — are they going too?'

'Yes.'

'You'll be able to keep in touch, though?'

'No, Mum, and I can't tell you where we're going either. But look, don't worry — '

'Don't worry?' Grace burst out, her voice breaking as a sob shook her. 'How will I not worry?'

'If I ever get the chance, I'll try and ring you, I promise. Till then, I have to go. I love you. Remember that.'

She'd ended the call, tears of anguish welling in her own eyes as she listened to her mother sobbing. What the hell had she got herself into? But how could she do anything else? Her life, her children's lives, could be in danger. At least the police had told her that they'd picked up Robert Wilmot and were holding him. 'You don't have to worry,' one of the officers assured her. 'He won't get bail.'

So that was one fear, at least, removed. However, there was still the other gang members to be concerned about, so the further they went from Birmingham the better. They were taken to a hotel several miles away from where they lived and, as promised, were given new names and new life histories, which they all had to memorise. Annabel became Kate, Melanie became Ellie, and Paul became Matt. Their surname would be Summers.

The children were outraged, especially Ellie. 'I'm not leaving. How can I? What will my friends think? I'll have to ring them and let them know.'

'You can't tell anyone where you're going,' the detective informed her. 'Or what your new names will be. This is very important.'

'Mum!' she'd wailed. 'Tell them!'

'Love, it's for your safety.'

'Why?' she furiously demanded.

'I-I saw someone kill someone else, and-and the killer saw me. He followed me home.'

'Oh my God!' she screamed melodramatically. 'Why did you do that?'

'I didn't choose to do it. It just happened.'

'Well, I'm not going. I'll live with Gran.' Ellie, as she now was, crossed her arms over her chest, her whole demeanour stiff with outrage and defiance.

'No, you won't. You're coming with me. Look — it'll be a lovely new life in Cornwall. Imagine — the beach on the doorstep.'

The detectives had asked her where she'd like to go, and with past holidays with Simon and the children and very occasionally her mother and sister in mind, she'd said, 'Cornwall — would that be possible?'

'Yes. We have a couple of safe houses there. It's always better if you move as far away as possible from your present home.'

'I don't want to go to the beach,' Ellie ranted. 'I hate sand. Nasty gritty stuff. And I won't have any friends down there. What will I do? I'll be sooo bored.'

The detective murmured, 'It won't be on the coast, I'm afraid. The house I'm thinking of is inland, not too far from Truro. Bodruggan. It's a small market town; hardly any tourists go there, so very little chance of anyone turning up and recognising you.'

After several hours of intensive coaching for all three of them, they finally had their stories memorised. They then piled into an unmarked vehicle, along with their bags, and set off on the long drive to Cornwall.

Ellie muttered at one point, 'I hope you packed my tablet.'

'No, I left all that sort of thing behind,' Kate said. 'I thought it best. You can't contact anyone.'

'Not even my friends?'

'No, Ellie.'

'My name's not Ellie!' she screamed. 'It's Mel!'

'It's Ellie from now on,' Kate gently but firmly told her.

They reached the small town in the early hours of the next morning, and once the officers had gone, it was Ellie who yet again did all the grumbling. 'Did you see that?' she moaned. 'What sort of pathetic place have you dragged us to?'

By this time, Kate was simply too weary to argue. 'Let's unpack what we need for now and go to bed. We'll sort everything out in the morning. I'm sure it'll all look better in daylight.'

# 3

But come the next morning, nothing did look any better, and certainly not to Ellie. She stared bleakly through the sitting-room window at the road outside, arms crossed over her narrow chest, the corners of her mouth turned down, the very picture of misery. And Kate had to admit that even for the end of March, it did look pretty dismal. The sky was a bruised grey, leaden with clouds as it was; the hedgerows and tree branches dripped with moisture after what had obviously been heavy rain overnight. It had left in its wake an impenetrable drizzle which misted the air and severely restricted their view of the surrounding countryside. But apart from the depressing weather, the house itself was completely isolated from the small town, which was, according to Kate's estimation the night before when they had driven through it, a good quarter of a mile away, maybe a little more.

'Where are the other houses, the other people?' Ellie grumbled. 'The neighbours? This looks totally boring. What will I do with myself?'

'I'm sure once we find our way round and get our bearings, it will all look heaps better.'

Kate tried very hard to sound upbeat and optimistic about the situation they found themselves in, despite her own reservations about it all. She realised she'd failed, however, when Ellie snorted with scorn and said, 'Well, you've got that right. It *is* a heap.'

But now, six weeks later, she did seem to be settling down. The grumbling had all but stopped, and she and Matt were attending the local school, where they'd both made friends.

Their liaison officer had visited several times, and he'd given Kate a dedicated phone number to call if needed, in the event that she believed she was in danger. He told her she must call the number, let the phone ring out twice before ending

45

the call, and then repeat the process. He'd know it was Kate and that she needed immediate help. He would instantly summon it for her.

She'd even found herself a job in a small dress shop in the town, Brenda's Boutique. It was in the main street, halfway along, and sandwiched between the greengrocer and the town's sole newsagent. Lining both sides of the road were several more shops: a butcher, a flower and gift shop, a Tesco Express, a unisex hairdressing salon, a bank, a very small post office that doubled as a second-hand bookshop. There were two pubs — The Ship and The Lugger, a café and an ice-cream parlour, and a fish and chip shop. There was even a small Indian restaurant. A modest library sat on one side of a fairly substantial church. On the other side of this was the school, with a surprisingly large playing field running alongside it. Interspersed amongst all of these, on both sides of the road, were a dozen or so small cottages, their grey slate roofs freckled with yellow and green lichen, each one sporting colourful hanging baskets on their granite walls. Where the main street, Fore Street, ended, the road narrowed into a high hedged lane, not much more than the width of a car, and which ultimately led to Truro.

Kate's job was part-time, three days a week — Wednesday, Thursday and Friday, ten till two, which suited her perfectly; she could spend the rest of the week with the children, when they weren't at school. But what made it even better was the fact that Brenda, the owner, had agreed to keep their arrangement casual and pay her in cash each week. She had raised an eyebrow at Kate's hesitant request before asking, 'Tax problems?'

'No,' Kate had cautiously replied, not being able to go into details. 'It's just easier. There isn't a branch of my bank here.'

The fact was, the allowance she was being given as part of the protection scheme wasn't sufficient for anything more than their most basic needs, so she was glad of the extra money. Her bank account had been frozen upon her entry into the witness protection scheme; not that there'd been much in it, in any case. She'd been living from week to week on her wages from her job as a receptionist at a solicitor's office five minutes from home. Simon had had a reasonable life insurance policy, but what money had been left after paying off the mortgage on the house had very quickly disappeared. Her mother had helped her out financially, as well as looking after the children once school closed for the day.

Still, the job at Brenda's had meant Kate could manage to buy herself a small hatchback car. It was cheap and second-hand, but it ran — rather noisily, it was true — and that was the main thing. She could drive the children to school and then get herself to work. Their three-bedroom cottage was, as Ellie had angrily pointed out, outside of the main town of Bodruggan, and a fair walk from the school. Morwenna lived another quarter of a mile on from Kate — away from the town, but still well within walking distance.

Gradually, the three of them were coming to terms with what had happened, and were indeed making new lives for themselves, and getting to know people. But more importantly, they were safe again. Or so Kate had assumed.

Then, the previous evening, she'd looked at Ross St. Clair and seen a man who had looked uncannily like Robert Wilmot, the killer. So much so that she'd truly believed it was him for a moment or two, before common sense had kicked in and she'd realised it couldn't possibly be him. Robert Wilmot was in prison, locked away, awaiting trial. At least, she hoped he was. A sensation of momentary panic persuaded her to ring her liaison officer, Bob Turpin, and make sure of that.

'There's no need to worry, Kate,' he told her with utter confidence. 'He's still in prison, I can assure you of that. He'd never get bail; he's too much of a flight risk.'

Kate breathed a huge sigh of relief and ended the call. Nevertheless, the incident had resurrected her fears, making her look over her shoulder for the next few days — which was how she gained an unexpected impression, a fleeting awareness, of someone following her; watching her. It came in the form of a tingling sensation in the back of her neck, a shiver down her spine; and when she turned, a momentary glimpse of a tall man sweeping around a corner. It was only a back view, and a very quick one at that, but it had revived disturbing memories of the killer.

Her first thought was, could it be Ross St. Clair? But why would he be following her? Maybe he'd just been passing and she'd caught a brief glimpse of him. Or was it possible that she'd identified the wrong man? Was an innocent man in prison because of her? Yet the police officer had told her Robert Wilmot was known to them as a member of a dangerous gang, so it had to have been him — didn't it? The fact that Ross St. Clair looked like him was pure coincidence. Her thoughts wouldn't stop turning over every possibility. Morwenna had told her he'd been in Australia. What if he'd lied to everyone and, in fact, he'd been in the midlands? No one would have known. But why would he be living in Cornwall, if he was a member of a Birmingham gang? He'd have remained in the midlands. It was the only thing that made sense. It hadn't been him. She'd identified the right man; the police had been sure of that. He was a known criminal. Everything fitted.

Finally, exasperated with her repeated and torturous anxieties and suspicions, Kate resolutely banished them all from her mind, determined to dispel her fears and doubts and insecurities once and for all, and get on with her life. So when Brenda offered her another hour a day in the shop, she enthusiastically accepted.

'As long as I can finish in time to collect the children from school.'

'That's fine,' Brenda assured her. 'Let's say ten till three. More money, of course.'

Brenda Tomlin was a good-looking woman and, Kate suspected, ten or eleven years older than herself. She had built herself a reputation over the past four years for having something a little different to offer the more discerning customer, which ensured that women came from all over the area to her shop before they went anywhere else. And, more importantly, they invariably bought something, which meant business was good and provided Brenda with a comfortable lifestyle. She'd divorced six years ago and had been forced to battle her ex-husband for her rightful share of their assets. He'd also had his own business, something to do with engineering, which Brenda had helped build up alongside him, and so she had felt perfectly entitled to have her share of whatever profits they'd generated over the previous years. After that, she was understandably bitter about men in general. So it wasn't surprising that that particular morning, she embarked upon one of her favourite topics of conversation, men. Her husband in particular.

'Apparently he's finally getting married again. Tosser! They're all tossers; can't trust one of them. I hope the poor cow knows what she's doing. If he treats her like he treated me ... Of course,' she went on, 'there are a few exceptions to that description. One in particular springs to mind.' She slanted a glance at Kate. 'Have you had the pleasure of meeting Ross St. Clair yet?'

'Yeah,' Kate said, 'a couple of weeks ago at Morwenna Lucas's. He and I were guests at her dinner party.'

Brenda's eyes glittered with feverish speculation. 'You didn't go with him, did you? You lucky beggar.'

'No. I met him for the first time there.'

'Oh, okay. So what did you think?'

'Of him?'

'Yes, of him.' Brenda rolled her eyes in mock impatience.

Kate didn't immediately answer. The truth was, she didn't know how friendly Brenda might be with him. She'd certainly never mentioned him before. She didn't want to say anything that Brenda might repeat to him. 'Um — well, he's quite good-looking, I suppose.'

'Quite good-looking — you suppose?'

Brenda scoffed. 'What's the matter with your eyesight, woman? He's bloody gorgeous. And sexy as hell to boot. I keep hoping he'll ask me out. Maybe you could introduce me.' She rolled her eyes lustfully. Kate laughed. 'He came in once with his daughter. He was buying her a dress for some sort of school function.'

'Yes, he told me he had a daughter. Cleo, isn't it?'

'Mmm. She looks a bit of a handful, frankly. She knew what she wanted and wouldn't accept anything else. They left, I'm sorry to say, empty-handed, though he was terribly apologetic about that. She'd had half of my stock off the hangers to try on, the little madam. I almost suggested he ask me out to compensate me for my time and trouble.' She gave a broad grin as she slowly licked her lips, her expression exactly the sort a cat would display as it gazed hungrily at a bowl of cream. 'I could give him a very good time — certainly help him to forget his troublesome daughter,' she drawled.

Kate couldn't help laughing again.

'Will you behave yourself? Anyway, I'm sure he can cope with a teenage girl. He seemed very sure of himself.' And that was an understatement if ever she'd made one. 'Very capable. I can't imagine much fazing him.' Although she recalled his admission of a few problems with Cleo — well, more than a few, if he were to be believed. So maybe he wasn't as capable as she'd just suggested.

'Yes, he does seem always very sure of himself,' Brenda agreed. 'And why wouldn't he be? He's worth megabucks, by all accounts.'

'Does he have any women friends?'

'By 'friend', I assume you mean mistress, lover — call it what you will.' Brenda's eyes gleamed with amusement. 'You're very diplomatic. As far as I know, he doesn't. But then, he's not one for broadcasting his private affairs, so who knows?' She shrugged.

'He lives just outside of the town, doesn't he?'

'You seem very interested in him.' Brenda cocked her head to one side.

'Not really. I'm just trying to learn about the town and its residents, that's all.'

'Okay. If you say so.'

However, something in the quality of her employer's stare told Kate she didn't believe her, not for a moment.

'So,' Brenda went on, 'just to help you out on that score — he lives in Bodruggan House, about three or four miles out of town. It's a massive place. It was originally owned by one of the tin-mining millionaires, but when that industry collapsed and disappeared they were forced to sell up. It's had several owners since then, Ross being the latest. He's lived there for about five years, I think. Have you seen it?'

'No, I haven't been out that way yet. In fact, I haven't ventured outside of Bodruggan.'

'Oh my. You'll have to take a drive by sometime. You can just see it from the road. It's pretty impressive. I've heard it's got eight bedrooms, all with their own bathrooms. Even more rooms downstairs, apparently. Acres and acres of land. There are stables — complete with horses, naturally; a swimming pool, tennis courts … you name it, it's there. I have heard he even has a helicopter to get around quickly. No sitting in traffic jams for him.'

'You seem to know a great deal about it all,' Kate said with her own smile of amusement now. 'Have you been inside the house?'

'No, worse luck. But well, you know what it's like in a small town. Everyone knows everyone else. And I know Beth Elliot, his housekeeper, as well as one of his daily cleaners.' Brenda raised an eyebrow at her. 'They keep me up to date with all the goings-on.'

Kate wondered if Ross knew his staff were gossiping about him. She couldn't imagine he'd be very pleased about that. 'What business is he in? It must be good to have made him so wealthy.'

'He's got his fingers in all sorts of pies. He's a genuine, gold-plated entrepreneur. He's got interests in the IT world. There's a large property development company

— St. Clair Enterprises. At the moment they're converting a huge old Victorian school in Truro into a leisure centre. He deals — very profitably, I believe — on the stock market, and all that's just a fraction of his business dealings. I believe there's a string of upmarket international hotels in his portfolio, too.'

'Goodness,' Kate said, tongue firmly lodged in her cheek, 'you do know a lot about him.'

Brenda eyed her suspiciously. 'Are you implying I'm nosey?'

'Of course not,' Kate guilelessly replied, all the while thinking that Brenda and Morwenna would make the perfect pair. Any morsel of gossip the one missed could be picked up by the other. They could then exchange their info and pass it on to other interested individuals — of which there would an entire legion, Kate was sure.

'Hmmm.' Brenda clearly didn't believe her, but she didn't seem to be taking offence. 'As I said, Bodruggan's a small place — Cornwall's a relatively small place, come to that — so things get round. And his daughter attends St. Mary's School, just outside the town, so she has friends there who talk as well.'

Kate belatedly felt uneasy despite her banter. She'd already concluded that gossip was rife here, which meant she and the children would have to be extra-cautious in all they did or said. One slip on their parts and the truth of who they were could come out — and that would spell complete disaster. She suspected they'd have to move again, which was the very last thing she wanted.

'That's a very expensive private school, isn't it?' Kate asked.

'Too right. Only the richest kids go there.'

'Where does the name St. Clair originate from? It's very unusual.'

'It is, isn't it? Sets them apart from the rest of us hoi-polloi. I did hear they're descended from an aristocratic French family called St.Clere, spelt C-l-e-r-e, who emigrated to England at the end of the eighteenth century to escape the guillotine. They then changed it to St. Clair, C-l-a-i-r, to sound less French, presumably; but how true that is, I have no idea. Anyway, someone then decided to change it again, to the more ordinary Sinclair. Less pretentious in their view, it was believed. They were also down on their fortunes at the time. One of the sons had gambled his way through most of the family's money. Then I think it was Ross's father — or was it his grandfather? I'm not sure. Anyway, whoever it was decided to restore the St. Clair version of the name, and it's been that way ever since.'

After that initially quiet period, several women entered the shop and started rifling through the racks of clothes, which meant both Brenda and Kate were kept busy. Three o'clock swiftly arrived. Kate, who had begun to feel fractionally more secure in this friendly little town, and with a sunny May morning beckoning, had impulsively decided to leave the car at home and walk to school and work that morning. Now she was heading off to pick up the two children. They were both waiting for her at the school gates, along with another girl who looked about Ellie's age.

'You're late,' Ellie crossly accused. 'Can Millie come home with us and have some tea? Her mum's had to go to Truro to visit someone in hospital. I said it would be okay.'

'Yes, of course it is,' Kate immediately agreed. 'Hello, Millie. I hope it's nothing too serious.'

'It's Granny. She's had a fall.'

'Oh dear. Well, let's get home then.' She eyed the sky, which was starting to cloud over. 'It looks as if we might be about to get some rain.'

'Why didn't you bring the car?' Ellie demanded. 'You might've known this would happen. We are in Cornwall, after all,' she scornfully concluded.

'Well, rain wasn't forecast this morning, and it was such glorious weather. If we hurry … '

'If we hurry,' Ellie sarcastically repeated — she was fast becoming a master of the art of irony — 'we'll still get wet.'

Oh good grief, another black mark on her copy book, Kate decided. Nothing she did seemed to please her daughter anymore. The young girl clearly blamed Kate for their forced move into the protection scheme. And, truth to tell, she herself was beginning to regret having reported what she'd seen that night. If only she'd kept quiet. She sighed. If she'd kept quiet, she and her children might by now be dead. But apart from that fear, she couldn't have brought herself to stay silent after witnessing such a horrific crime. She'd always been intrinsically honest, even as a girl, an ingrained instinct invariably compelling her to confess to any wrongdoing, either at home or at school. She recalled the many times she'd been castigated by her friends, her sister especially. 'Just keep your mouth shut,' Lizzie had repeatedly told her. 'You're too honest for your own good — and mine,' she'd add if she'd been involved in whatever the trouble had been — which was quite often.

The rain, which had started falling just

moments ago, was intensifying, and in the process drenching them all. Kate suspected her hair was plastered to her head and probably hanging in rat's tails; even her underwear felt wet. The three children looked as dejected as she felt. 'Let's have a race,' she said, trying to inject some fun into the whole sorry business. But Ellie was having none of that.

'Are you crazy? How can we race in this? It's pouring. We can barely see ahead.'

All of a sudden, Kate became aware of a large vehicle pulling up to one side of them. A horn blasted out. Startled, they all stopped moving and turned to look behind them. A white Range Rover had pulled up to the kerbside, and in its driving seat Kate saw, of all people, Ross St. Clair. He was grinning broadly through the windscreen at them. Alongside him sat a very pretty teenage girl. This must be Cleo, Kate decided.

Ross wound his window down and called, 'I thought it was you. Can I offer you all a lift home? We're going this way, so it wouldn't be any trouble.'

'Yes, please,' Ellie instantly responded. Without a moment's hesitation, she took a couple of quick steps sideways, opened the rear door, and leapt up inside.

'Ellie … ' Kate began.

'There's one eminently sensible girl,' Ross laughed, completely ignoring her word of caution to her daughter. 'Kate? Are you coming?'

'Well … ' Ross St. Clair was the last person she wanted to be indebted to for anything, even something as minor as a lift in the rain. 'It's not much further to home.'

'Oh, come on. You're absolutely soaked, all of you.' He grinned at her. 'I've seen drier frogs!'

She glared at him. Was he comparing her to a frog?

'That didn't come out right, did it?' His maddening grin broadened even further.

'No,' she muttered, 'it certainly didn't.'

'Oh, get in, Mum,' Ellie called in distinct exasperation. 'What's the problem?'

Ross had climbed down from his seat

by this time, his expression one of almost repentance. 'Sorry,' he said. He then placed both hands on each side of her waist and unceremoniously hoisted her up into the vehicle. He'd have handled a sack of coal with more care, she indignantly decided. It was utterly mortifying. He then lifted Matt in and turned to do the same with Millie. After which, having got his own way — why had she expected anything else? Kate wondered irritably — he climbed back into the driving seat and said, 'Right. Honeysuckle Cottage, isn't it?', completely disregarding his daughter's hacked-off stare.

The man was a complete autocrat, Kate decided; nothing more than a dictator. And if it wasn't for that fact that Ellie would almost certainly refuse to do so, Kate would open the rear door and climb out, ordering the three children to do the same. So it was with considerable reluctance that she muttered, 'Yes, towards the end of Beech Road.' He'd clearly overheard her giving her address to Mags the other evening.

'I know it.' And he toed the accelerator and took off, the puddles of water that were quickly building up on the road surface splashing noisily round the tyres as he did so. 'I have to say, you do seem very fond of walking,' he remarked, deliberately and ironically referring to her refusal of the lift home that he'd offered her at Morwenna's.

'I do,' she stiffly conceded, 'when the weather's good. Otherwise, I drive. This is us, just up ahead on the left.'

He pulled to a halt in front of the cottage and peered at it through the passenger window. 'Pretty. I've never really looked at it before.'

And it *was* pretty. An abundance of gloriously scented tangerine honeysuckle rampaged up the cream-washed wall, attractively framing the pale blue front door. Neat white and pink rose bushes lined one side of the short driveway, behind which lay a flower bed, and then behind that, a thick hedgerow, which butted against the side of the house and divided the garden from the field beyond.

On the other side was a narrow stretch of lawn, along which ran a fence with a gate at a right angle to it, again meeting the wall of the house, thus providing the sole access from the front to the rear garden.

'We like it,' Kate said.

'No, we don't,' Ellie brusquely argued. 'It's smaller than our last house, and in the middle of nowhere.'

'Only very slightly smaller,' Kate corrected her. 'Come on, everybody out.'

Throughout the short journey and then the brief conversation, Cleo hadn't uttered a single word. Now she disparagingly remarked, 'It's very small. How do the four of you cope? Bunk beds, is it?'

Kate felt a stab of irritation. However, all she said was, 'It's only three of us. Millie's visiting.'

'Is that your car on the drive?' Ross asked, his raised eyebrow indicating suppressed amusement; even, maybe, a touch of disdain. For the second time, Kate experienced intense irritation. What was it with these two? Who did they think they were, criticising what others had? Mind you, she recalled Mags's air of disapproval. Maybe it was a local trait.

'Does it go okay?' Ross added, more seriously.

'Of course it goes,' Kate tersely said. 'It's all I need. It gets me from A to B.'

Cleo gave a loud snort. 'What about the rest of the alphabet? Does it get you there too?' She sniggered.

Definitely like father, like daughter, Kate concluded. Ellie threw the door open, but Ross had pre-empted her. He was already standing there, his hands reaching out to help her down.

Kate hadn't seen him move. She'd been far too busy studying Cleo. Brenda's verdict on the girl being a handful was definitely the right one. Kate wouldn't want to have to deal with her on a daily basis. Ellie was a walk in the park in comparison — well, a tiring walk, but still easier to cope with, she imagined, than Cleo. The girl was arrogant and unlikable.

Ellie took Ross's hands and politely said 'thank you' before smiling warmly up at him, Kate saw. So even a ten-year-old girl wasn't immune to his good looks. That didn't make her feel any better. Was it only she who could see through what she suspected was his superficial charm? She was sure that beneath it was an unpleasantly dictatorial temperament. If he didn't get his own way, that smile would quickly transform itself into a bad-tempered scowl. She'd already glimpsed the first signs of a temper when she'd refused to do what he wanted her to.

Matt and Millie quickly scrambled past Kate to follow Ellie. Finally, Kate had no option but to slide across the back seat and ungraciously accept Ross's help. 'Thanks,' she muttered. She then glanced up at him and encountered eyes that were dancing with amusement and lips that were turned up at the corners.

He lowered his head so his mouth was on a level with her ear and murmured, 'Have you changed your mind about joining me one evening for dinner?'

As if Cleo had heard this, she turned her head and said, 'Dad, we have to go.

My lesson's at four o'clock.'

'She's having riding lessons,' Ross said. 'The school's not far from here.'

'Da-ad. Please, come on.'

'Okay, okay.' Ross turned back to Kate. 'You haven't answered my question.'

'That's right, I haven't. I haven't changed my mind, no. I don't go out much in the evenings.'

'Why not? You're hardly in your dotage.' His tone was a critical one.

Exasperation flared within her. 'It's the children. Until they're more settled … '

Ellie was beginning to exhibit noticeable impatience too. And no wonder. The rain wasn't quite as heavy as it had been, but it was still coming down fairly hard. 'I'm getting very wet here, and so's Millie.' Even Matt, usually so patient, was jogging from one foot to the other.

'As you can hear, I need to get them all inside. So, thank you for the lift.'

'Okay.' He sounded resigned. The trouble was, his facial expression didn't reflect that impression. That signalled a definite determination not to let this

70

matter go. She recalled his whispered, 'I always get my way in the end.' Well, this time he wasn't going to.

'I'll be seeing you,' he finally remarked.

*Not if I see you first,* was her silent response to that.

# 4

Later that evening, something happened to resurrect Kate's previous vague unease. To save Millie's mother the trouble, she'd agreed to run the girl home. It had still been raining heavily; so heavily, in fact, that even though it was only eight fifteen, it was virtually dark.

It was as she and the children were returning to Honeysuckle Cottage once more that she became aware of a car behind her; a large car with headlights that blazed, dazzling her in the rear-view mirror. The driver repeatedly closed the gap between them, noisily toeing the accelerator, before widening it again, until it eventually started to feel like deliberate intimidation rather than someone merely displaying impatience. Or was she letting her imagination run away with her, Kate wondered, and it was simply someone keen to overtake? Maybe they were late for an engagement of some sort. But taking into account the narrowness of the lane — a single car's width — why was the driver being so damned aggressive towards her? It wasn't as if she could pull over to allow whoever it was to get by. High hedges lined the lane on each side, which only served to intensify her sense of being under intense pressure. Again, she heard the roar of the engine as the driver toed the accelerator. For the umpteenth time she glanced in the mirror, but it was impossible to see who it was in the vehicle, other than that he was a man. A big man.

Her heart began to hammer as disturbing memories of the occasions she'd sensed she was being followed made their presence felt; the times she'd caught glimpses of a disappearing back, a man's back. Was this the same person? Had someone recognised her? Was that likely? She was, after all, miles away from Birmingham. And who would be trying to scare her, in any case? Then she remembered the police officer's warning — that even if the killer was in prison, his accomplices could be a threat to her. Could this be a member of Robert Wilmot's gang? Had they somehow traced her, and were now trying to intimidate and scare her into refusing to give evidence in court? That was why she'd been placed in witness protection — to stop this sort of thing happening, as well as to keep her safe from harm; and to make sure she could give her evidence and convict Robert Wilmot. But how could they have found her? Her whereabouts couldn't have been leaked; nobody knew where she was.

She stared into the mirror again. If she could just recognise the model of car, it might provide a clue as to who the driver was. But it was hopeless. The vehicle was too close — practically nudging the rear of her hatchback, in fact. A deliberate tactic to stop her from identifying it? From seeing the number plate? It was at that juncture that she felt the beginnings of real fear. He could crush her small car; ram her into the hedge — through it, even. They could all be seriously injured.

'Mummy, what's that car doing?'

It was Matt. He and Ellie were in the rear seat. He was half-turned around, straining upwards to stare through the rear window. He sounded frightened, and with good reason. Her children would be first in line for serious injury.

'Is he going to bang into us?'

'No, darling. Just hang on. We're almost out of this lane, and then he'll be able to pass us. He's just a very rude driver.'

Up ahead of her, she glimpsed the first glimmer of street lights. They were approaching the town and its two-way main street. Keen now for the journey to be over, she put her foot down on the accelerator — at the exact second that a car pulled out of a side road, mere inches in front of her. She slammed her foot onto the brake, her tyres screaming as she skidded on the wet surface, and she fought to bring the car to a halt instead of ending up in the hedgerow; which, for a tense moment, had looked more than likely. The driver didn't seem to see her, and with no sign of any remorse or apology, raced away towards the lights of the town. The car behind also revved loudly and finally managed to speed past her.

Kate began to breathe again; rather quickly, it was true, but at least she was breathing. She'd genuinely started to fear for their safety, especially when the other car had leapt out in front of her. She'd actually wondered for a split second whether it was some sort of tactic, a trap into which she'd blindly driven, to force her to stop in order to harm her and her children.

But now, in the aftermath and with the reassuring sight of the houses and shops just ahead of her, she decided she'd been overreacting, because both vehicles had vanished. Even so, she regretted not being able to identify the model that had been behind her. It had been big and dark in colour, she had been able to see that. Black, maybe? It could have been a Mercedes or a BMW.

But her ordeal wasn't over, because both children were now crying with fright. 'Mum!' Ellie screamed. 'What on earth just happened? You almost crashed the car.'

'I-I'm not sure.'

'Was that car following us?'

'I'm sure he wasn't.' But in actual fact, she wasn't at all sure of that. She didn't want to frighten the children any more than they already were, however, so she said as calmly as she could, 'He was just impatient to get past.'

She drove slowly back to the cottage as she struggled to work out exactly what had just happened, and if she should be afraid. Could it have been some sort of warning? One that, if unheeded, would mean she and her children would meet with some sort of accident?

$$\star \quad \star \quad \star$$

Kate lay in bed that night, wondering if she should ring Bob and report what had happened. The more she considered the evening's events, the more convinced she became that she had been followed; that someone, a man, had set out to terrify her. However, she decided to wait and see if anything else happened first. If she reported that she was seriously frightened, mightn't the protection-scheme people want to move her again? She wasn't sure what the procedure was in such an event. But that was the last thing she wanted, and the last thing Ellie or Matt would accept.

★　★　★

The next day, she and Brenda were kept busy in the shop, and that drove all else from Kate's mind. Until that evening.

The children were in bed, and she was watching a repeat of her favourite detective program, Vera, and sipping a glass of wine, when the doorbell chimed. Nervously she sat upright, memories of the evening before and the scary drive back from Millie's house still terrifyingly vivid.

The bell rang again, longer and more insistently this time. She put her glass down and stood up. She'd have to answer it, though who could be visiting her at this time she couldn't imagine. It was gone nine o'clock.

She walked to the door and called, 'Who is it?'

No one answered. Her nervousness deepened. If it was one of her friends, they would have replied. She called again, 'I'm not opening the door until you tell me who's out there.'

'Special delivery.'

Special delivery, at this time of the evening? Gingerly she opened the door a mere inch, just enough for her to peer out. A man stood there, holding a large box.

'Can you sign, please?' He held out an electronic pad and pen. Reassured by the ordinariness of the question, Kate pulled the door open and signed his pad. 'Thanks. Have a good evening.' He then handed her the box and left again. He was driving a white van.

Frowning, Kate carried the box into the kitchen, placed it on the worktop, and stared down at it. She hadn't ordered anything. She knew she was a bit at sixes and sevens at the moment, but she wouldn't have forgotten something like that, surely.

She pulled pair of scissors from a drawer and swiftly cut through the brown parcel tape that secured the lid of the box. Then she opened it.

She gasped. This was most definitely not intended for her ... or was it? A chill shivered all the way through her. Inside the box lay a wreath of flowers. All white flowers. She identified chrysanthemums, roses, lilies — the flower of death, she'd always called it — and carnations. They were interspersed with glossy dark green leaves. Laurel leaves, she thought.

It was a funeral wreath. There was no doubt about that.

She searched for a card — anything, scrabbling around the flowers with fingers that quivered. There was nothing there. Carefully she lifted the wreath from the box and placed it to one side. She could see no form of identification anywhere.

Nothing to indicate who'd sent it, or even from which flower shop it had come. No name, no phone number that she could ring to find out who was behind the mysterious delivery.

She stared at it again, one thought uppermost in her mind. Could this again be some sort of threat — something to reinforce her steadily growing sense of intimidation, of menace? She considered her suspicion that she was being followed round town. Then there was the car last night, pursuing her, practically pushing her through the lane. Were they warnings to her? Talk and you die? Because that was certainly what this wreath suggested. It was something to be placed on a grave. Her grave?

She could hear the soundtrack of Vera coming from the sitting room. The last thing she needed now was to watch a crime show. It all of a sudden felt much too close to her own situation for comfort. She went into the sitting room and turned off the television.

She stood in the centre of the room. If

she was being genuinely threatened with harm, who was behind it? It couldn't be Robert Wilmot. He was in prison. It must be someone working on his behalf. Someone who, against all the odds, had discovered her whereabouts. But how? She'd contacted no one from her old life. Nor had the children; she was as sure of that as she could be. Mind you, Ellie could be pretty rebellious; but even so, she wouldn't be that silly. Kate had told her over and over how risky it would be to contact any of her friends.

And it was then that one name flashed into her head: Ross St. Clair. He knew where she lived — he'd driven her home the day before. But — and the thought wouldn't be ignored — could this be the reason for his pursuit of her? Not because he was attracted to her, but because he was trying to get close to her; close enough to give him the opportunity to harm her? Somehow though, as deeply as he exasperated her, she simply couldn't believe it of him. He seemed so genuine. All right, he could be maddeningly self-assured — arrogant, even. But murder? It didn't feel right.

She returned to the kitchen, her mind made up, telling herself the wreath had been a mistake; nothing more sinister than a wrong delivery. It wasn't meant for her. She had to believe that, for the sake of her sanity.

She picked the wreath up and went outside to the bin, where she threw it inside. There. End of. She made a wiping motion with her hands. She would now put the whole thing from her mind. Banish her lingering suspicions and fears. Refuse to give them space in her head. The two events happening so close together had been coincidental, nothing more than that.

She returned to the sitting room and switched the television back on. She wasn't going to waste any more of her time speculating and worrying about what might be. She was going to get on with her life and make the most of what she had: a home, her children, a job she loved. There were thousands of people who'd give their all for those things.

But her resolution was easier made than carried out. Sleep that night proved maddeningly elusive. And when she did manage to drop off, her slumber was punctuated by disturbing dreams. In each of them, she was being chased by a mysterious hooded man. A man who had pale amber eyes.

*   *   *

Brenda took one look at her the next morning and said, 'Wow! What kept you up last night? Or should I ask — who?'

Kate longed to be able to tell her the truth; to confide her worries, her fears to someone. But she knew she couldn't, and certainly not to Brenda. Her employer, as good-natured as she was, wasn't the most discreet of women, and she wouldn't be able to resist sharing such an exciting and intriguing morsel of gossip with the rest of the town. So all Kate said was, 'No one kept me up. I couldn't sleep, end of story.' Then she shrugged as if to indicate that it wasn't anything out of the ordinary.

'You need a good night out if you ask me,' Brenda declared. 'How about you and I hit the hot spots?'

'Where are those, then?' Kate sarcastically asked.

Brenda sighed melodramatically. 'Don't be rude about our little town. Actually, I was thinking more about Truro. There are a few tempting places there.'

'I'm really not into clubbing.'

'No, nor me. I was thinking of a nice little pub-cum-bistro that I know. We could have a nice cocktail or two and then some supper. How about it?'

Kate sighed longingly. It did sound tempting. It felt like decades since she'd had a good evening out, apart from her and Morwenna's occasional foray to The Ship. And she didn't classify that as a good evening out. It was just a glass of wine and a pub snack.

'I'd have to find a babysitter,' she said.

'Doesn't Morwenna's eldest do it for you now and again? Pattie? Ask her. In fact, we could ask Morwenna to come too. A girls' night out.'

'Do you know, that sounds great.'

And it did. It was Friday, after all, and she didn't work Saturdays. Another local woman came in then. Kate preferred to spend the weekend with the children. So it wouldn't matter if she ... well, over-indulged a little. Not that she was ever much of a drinker. A large of glass of red wine was usually more than enough. Any more than that and she had serious trouble focusing, let alone walking.

'Okay, then. Give Morwenna a ring and fix it up. I'm sure she'll be game. Pattie can always take Imogen with her to yours if Brett's away or out.'

Pattie and Imogen were Morwenna's two daughters, sixteen and fourteen respectively. Pattie always came to the cottage when Kate and Morwenna went out. They never went anywhere expensive. Morwenna seemed to instinctively know that Kate didn't have money to spare.

Morwenna was just as eager to join them as Brenda had predicted. 'Absolutely — count me in,' she said. 'Brett's away till

Sunday sometime, so I'll bring the girls round to yours at seven o'clock and we'll pick Brenda up and go on from there.'

'Okay.' Kate now turned to Brenda. 'Brett's away, as you thought he might be, but Morwenna's keen to come.'

Brett did a lot of travelling in the course of his work. Mind you, it also looked as if he made a considerable amount of money. The luxury of their large detached house reinforced that impression. Kate wasn't clear about what he did; something in advertising, she thought. Even Morwenna didn't seem to know that much about it, but she seemed happy enough with her way of life. Kate had never heard her complain about her husband's frequent absences; she simply got on with things. And whatever he did, it earned enough to provide them with an extremely comfortable lifestyle. Certainly, Morwenna didn't need a job in order to make ends meet — which could account for her ready acceptance of the amount of time he spent away from her.

Ellie and Matt, of course, were

delighted with the news when she told them. They loved Pattie; she enthusiastically joined in all their games, no matter how childish they were. And to have Imogen there as well was little short of being heaven in their view.

There was only one niggling drawback, as far as Kate was concerned. As hard as she tried, she couldn't completely rid herself of the suspicion that she might have some sort of stalker; or, even more worrying, that he might be out to do her or her children harm — especially if he was a member of Robert Wilmot's gang. But, as she repeatedly asked herself, how could he have managed to locate her? No one knew where she was.

She told herself over and over that she had no real evidence that anyone was stalking her. Each incident could be put down to some sort of mistake: the fleeting glimpses of a man in the town, simply a passerby in a hurry to get somewhere; the car chase in the lane that, as she'd told herself at the time, was most likely nothing more dangerous than an impatient motorist. As for the wreath ... well, as she'd decided at the time, a wrong delivery. She was in all probability making a mountain out of someone else's incompetence and lack of manners — events, in other words, that were no more than ordinary incidents; the kinds of things that happened in normal day-to-day life.

For the umpteenth time, she told herself it was more than time to put it all out of her mind, and instead concentrate on what to wear for her girls' night out. But that was also a problem. She'd left many of her clothes behind in Birmingham, only bringing what she deemed essential items with her. Nevertheless, a shiver of excitement quivered through her. The mere opportunity to get out of Bodruggan was a thrilling one. She and Morwenna didn't bother changing clothes for the local pub and were, more often than not, back home again by nine thirty. Kate was determined to make more of an effort this evening and dress accordingly. Knowing Brenda, she'd be done up to the nines, and Kate had no desire to look like a poverty-stricken drab relation.

Depressingly, though, and not unexpectedly, when she viewed her collection of clothes, nothing at all leapt out at her. There was the dress she'd worn to Morwenna's dinner party, but other than that all she could find were various pairs of trousers, ranging from cotton crops to slightly smarter full-length, linen. As for tops, there were plain T-shirts or tunics.

Eventually, she regarded the heap on the bed and finally settled on the only acceptable garment she owned: the dress, again. However, it did suit her, the blue complementing her Titian-coloured hair and hazel eyes. The only problem with it was the dipping neckline, which exposed a considerable amount of cleavage. She eyed it doubtfully. She didn't want any men who were around interpreting that as some sort of come-on, as Ross St. Clair evidently had. At least she wouldn't need to worry about him this evening. He almost certainly wouldn't be wherever it was they were going.

*Forget him*, she told herself. *Look for-ward to the evening ahead, and the fun that simply being with your two friends will bring.* Fun that had been in very short supply of late.

With that, she pulled the dress from its hanger and slipped it on, and from then on everything went according to plan. Morwenna arrived with her two daughters, looking very glamorous. She'd piled her raven-black hair up onto her head, leaving just one or two curly strands to hang free around her ears. She was a petite woman, five feet two max, and slender, with cat-like features, even down to her slanting, strikingly green eyes. She made the taller Kate feel like a carthorse alongside her, especially when she was wearing four-inch heels, as she was this evening. Morwenna could be a flirt with the right man, but Kate had never once questioned her devotion or complete loyalty to Brett.

Pattie and Imogen were quickly settled in, and Ellie already had several boxed games laid out ready to play, so the two women wasted no time in driving to Brenda's house to collect her. Brenda, running true to form, and despite her vehement denial to Kate that they would be going to a club, was dressed for exactly that. She was wearing a top low enough to render Kate's positively demure, and a skin-tight leather skirt that stopped a good six inches above her knees. Her honey-blonde hair was piled up on top of her head, back-combed and lacquered to within an inch of its life. As for her makeup, that was expertly applied to enhance her deep blue eyes and full-lipped mouth.

'Wow!' Morwenna exclaimed.

Brenda cheekily did a twirl for them, saying, 'Well, I don't do this very often.'

'Do what?' Kate asked with a sinking feeling.

'Go out on the pull. So I want to make the most of it.'

Every one of Kate's fears seemed about to be realised. She felt a stab of horror. 'On the pull? Is that what we're doing? Only, I don't think ...'

'Not you, lovey. Me.' Brenda grinned. 'I have to grab my chances when I get the opportunity, and you never know who we'll bump into.' She gave a long, slow wink at the two other women.

Kate looked desperately at Morwenna, who was grinning every bit as widely as Brenda was. So, Kate decided, no help there then. However, when Morwenna murmured, 'Looks like we're set to be just the onlookers tonight then, Kate,' she realised she wasn't on her own and felt instantly reassured.

'Indeed — as far as I'm concerned, at any rate,' Kate responded.

Morwenna eyed her. 'So, has Ross been in touch since the dinner? He looked totally smitten to me.'

Kate blinked at her. 'Smitten? That wasn't the way it looked to me.'

'Oh.' Morwenna's eyes sparkled. 'How did it look to you, then?'

'As if he was removing all of my cloth-ing, item by item,' Kate bit out. 'And, what's more, relishing every damned minute of it — including the end result of such outrageous cheek — my scarlet face.'

'That's Ross for you. He's harmless, believe me.' Morwenna laughed.

'Harmless?' Kate bit out. 'If he's harmless, I must be very out of touch. I've seen snakes less harmless than him. A rattlesnake would be less of a risk.'

'Never mind you being out of touch,' Morwenna scoffed, completely ignoring the gibe about the rattlesnake. 'Has he been in touch?'

'Well, if you can call giving me and the kids a lift home the other day being in touch, then yes, I suppose he has. We were caught out in all that rain.'

'Ho, ho. And?' She looked expectantly at Kate.

'And nothing. He dropped us off and took Cleo for her riding lesson.'

Morwenna made no attempt to conceal her disappointment. She frowned; even the corners of her mouth turned down. 'That doesn't sound like Ross. He's not usually backward in coming forward.'

'Well, he did ask me out.'

'And?' Morwenna practically screamed the word.

'And I said no, I wasn't interested.'

Morwenna regarded her then as if she'd lost her mind. 'You're not interested?' she scoffed. 'How the hell could you not be interested in Ross St. Clair? He's got it all — good looks, money, fab house. Are you mad, woman? I thought you were just playing hard to get at my house. You know, playing it cool, just to whet his considerable appetite — if you know what I mean.' She gave a wicked smile.

'No, I wasn't play-acting. I actually was cool. He's not my type. I prefer to concentrate on my children.'

This time it was Brenda who burst out, 'My God, I have to agree with Morwenna. You must be insane. Not your type? Christ! I wish he'd ask me out. I'd bite his bloody hand off, and that would just be for starters. I'd very quickly move on to the tastier bits.' She licked her lips with unmistakable lust.

Kate, deciding it was more than time she ended this particular conversation, briskly said, 'Shall we go?'

Within fifteen minutes they were parking in Truro and on their way to the pub-bistro that Brenda had recommended. The second they were inside, Kate knew it had been a grave mistake to come. It was clearly a meeting place for single people — rich single people, by the look of it, though that didn't disguise the fact that they were all here on the lookout for a partner of some sort.

'Come on,' Brenda eagerly said. 'There's a free table over in the corner. You two grab it and I'll get us a bottle of wine.'

It wasn't until Kate and Morwenna were halfway across the floor and heading for the empty table that Kate realised, with a heaving lurch of her heart, that her conviction that Ross St. Clair wouldn't be here had been way off the mark. For the first person she saw was him, sitting with another man.

What the hell was he doing in a place like this? Mind you, he could reasonably ask her the same question, and probably would, given half a chance. There was no denying that this place was the obvious venue to get yourself a date, and she'd told him quite categorically that she didn't date.

# 5

Just as Kate feared he would, he spotted the two of them a couple of seconds after she saw him. She watched as an eyebrow lifted and arched, right before he murmured something to his companion. The other man swivelled his head and also watched them as they walked towards the empty table. Although Kate averted her gaze, she distinctly heard a long, low wolf whistle. She promptly glared at Ross, her expression one of accusation, only to have him shake his head at her, indicating he wasn't the one responsible. And, to be honest, she couldn't imagine a man like him doing such a thing. It must have been his companion, because she couldn't mistake the expression of lust upon his face as he watched her and Morwenna moving towards their table.

It wasn't until the three of them were seated, Kate deliberately positioning herself so that she didn't have to look at Ross, and they were all laughing at an outrageous remark from Brenda, that he strode across to them. 'Hello. How nice to see you all. Unexpected,' he drily remarked, 'but good.'

Kate frowned as she took a large mouthful of her drink. What the hell did that mean? And how did their presence here have anything to do with him? Huh! He probably didn't approve — though it was perfectly acceptable for him to be in such a place, of course, so large was his ego.

'Brett away again?' he asked Morwenna.

'Yes. Germany this time. He's back on Sunday. And you know how it is ...' She gave a mischievous grin. 'While the cat's away, the mouse will go out to play.'

'Oh, I most certainly do,' he said, something in his tone indicating that maybe his wife had played around behind his back. He turned his head then to look at Kate. 'I hope you didn't end up too wet the other day.'

'A little damp, but it wasn't too bad, thank you. The frog successfully turned back into a woman again,' she sarcastically added. She was aware of both Morwenna and Brenda staring at her in astonishment, but she didn't respond. Instead, she fixed a cool smile onto her lips and waited for whatever he decided to say next.

'A slip of the tongue,' he glibly excused himself. 'No one could possibly look at you and see a frog.'

'Um — what's this about frogs?' Brenda was looking intrigued. 'Is that a change to the fairy tale? Wasn't it a prince who had been turned into a frog, and a princess who kissed him?' When no one answered her, she went on with dogged determination, 'What I want to know is, in this version, did a handsome prince turn up and deliver the kiss? I have to say, though, if he didn't, he most certainly has now. Better late than never, eh?' She smiled provocatively at Ross.

But Ross didn't seem to hear her, much less notice the smile. He was far too engaged in staring at Kate. As for Kate, she was waiting for whatever was coming next. It didn't take long.

'You managed to find a sitter again, then?' His smile was as cool as her own had been.

'Morwenna's daughter Pattie is doing the honours.'

Heavy lids hooded the amber eyes. He really was a very good-looking man, Kate couldn't help thinking. Under any other circumstances, she would be tempted to accept his invitation to go out, despite her longstanding aversion to handsome men. But her particular situation precluded it. She was determined not to get involved with a man, and certainly not this man, someone she wouldn't be able to whole-heartedly trust.

'Not totally impossible to get out for an evening, then?' he said. 'Or is it that you're here tonight to find someone more acceptable to you?' He glanced around at all the unaccompanied men.

'No, I'm here with my friends to have an evening out. There's no other motive.'

She met his gaze head-on. 'I'm still not in the market for dating anyone.'

His expression hardened momentarily, but it didn't stop him asking, 'Would you mind if Dan and I joined you all?' He glanced towards the other two women. 'It sounds as if you're having far more fun than we are.'

'Would the fox refuse to eat the chicken?' Brenda saucily asked. 'Of course we don't mind.'

'Dan?' Morwenna said.

'Yeah, he's a good friend of mine.'

'How's Cleo?' Brenda chipped in.

Ross turned to her. 'Sorry, I don't think I … ' He gave a puzzled frown, clearly not recognising her.

Brenda, looking a bit miffed, hastily said, 'Owner of the only dress shop in Bodruggan, Brenda's Boutique?'

'Oh, yes. I came in once with Cleo. She's fine, out on a sleepover tonight.'

'Ooh, leaving Daddy free to play?' She smiled up at him from beneath lowered eyelashes. It was a provocative gesture, designed to let him know she was willing to join him.

Ross grinned as he allowed his glance to move lower, taking in the abundance of flesh that was on show. 'You could say that, I suppose. Not that *playing* is really my forte anymore.'

Brenda pouted. 'Shame, because I was hoping to find a playmate tonight.'

Kate stared at her, dismayed to feel a sharp piercing of jealousy as she noted the manner in which Ross was regarding Brenda — with more than a little interest, belatedly. Kate silently snorted. If that wasn't just typical of a man. Couldn't resist a sexy come-on. They really were pathetic. She waited for his acceptance of Brenda's invitation, not bothering to hide her disgust.

But all Ross did was glance sideways at Kate before giving a small smile and turning back to Brenda. 'Well, I'm extremely sorry to disappoint you, but I do have other plans.' Whereupon he slanted a second glance at Kate; it was a supremely satisfied glance.

Kate couldn't mistake his meaning

— that his plans concerned her. He couldn't have detected her pang of jealousy, could he? She wouldn't be surprised. She felt her face begin to glow as embarrassment swamped her. Her mother had always said her every thought was written plainly on her face. Why couldn't she be like other people and cultivate a little impenetrability? She'd always envied that ability.

Brenda gave a 'hmph' of disappointment and said, 'Shame about that, but never mind. Call your friend over.'

Ross beckoned to Dan, at the same time dragging two spare chairs to their table. 'So, Brenda, how's business?'

'Good. Did you know that Kate's joined me for three days a week?'

'I didn't, no. I'll make sure I call in, then, and say hello.' His gaze turned to Kate. 'Which three days are you working?'

The question caught her unawares. 'Uh —Wednesday, Thursday and Friday.'

'I'll have to check out what you've got.' The words were lazily drawled and loaded with sexual innuendo, as his gaze briefly lowered to her revealing neckline.

Kate tightened her lips. 'Oh, nothing that you'd be interested in, I'm sure.'

'Are you? How do you know what I'd be interested in?'

Her two friends were now silently listening to this. Morwenna seemed especially interested. 'Oh.' Kate made a great play of guileless surprise. 'Are you a cross-dresser, then?'

'No, I was referring to Cleo — naturally.' His face was alight with amusement. 'She's always on the lookout for something out of the ordinary. Can you offer her anything like that?'

But if the question stumped Kate, Brenda was more than ready to step in. 'I'm sure we can. We have a lot of teenagers coming in. I can usually find them something. We try to cater for all age groups.'

'It's a date, then.' Although Ross's remark was aimed at Brenda, he was looking at Kate. Again, she couldn't mistake his meaning. He would be coming to see her, specifically.

Brenda hid a smile, but did manage a sly wink at Kate and a perfectly audible, 'You've scored, gal,' to Kate's further embarrassment.

Kate stoically ignored her friend's remark — she certainly wasn't going to grace it with a reply — and instead took a hefty slug of her wine, which predictably sped straight to her head and induced a momentary dizziness. She was completely unprepared for Ross to nudge his chair in between her and Brenda, as Dan did the same between Brenda and Morwenna. After which, to her dismay, she felt Ross slide his arm along the back of her chair, thus ensuring that he was physically touching her. She immediately jerked forward, away from him, and rested her elbows on the table top, only to slant a swift glance at him — which meant she saw the exact second his mouth broadened into a knowing grin. He was fully aware of how deeply he was affecting her. God, he was so smug. It was bloody infuriating.

He tilted his head towards hers. 'Do I

make you feel uncomfortable?'

'Not at all,' she curtly retaliated. 'Why on earth would you think that?'

'Well, could it be something to do with the way you immediately sat forward — almost sliding onto the table, in fact — the second I put my arm behind you.'

His eyes gleamed at her; they were illuminated by the minute gold flecks that she'd glimpsed once before. She wondered what it was they signalled. Irritation? Pleasure? Amusement, probably, at her childish behaviour. Why couldn't she take these sorts of things in her stride as Morwenna would, or Brenda? They'd just laugh it off, and add some sort of smart remark.

'You needn't worry,' he went on. 'I'm not about to make a grab for you.'

'I should hope not.' She closed her eyes momentarily. Now she sounded like some sort of prim maiden aunt. Could things get any worse?

'I wouldn't be that obvious.' The glints shone brighter.

She stared at them, almost mesmerised.

'Really?'

'Really. But I wish you'd agree to come out to dinner with me.'

'Are you going to be eating here?'

'Yes. Are you?'

'Yes. So that could be considered having dinner with you, couldn't it?' And now it was her turn to give a smug smile.

He frowned at her. 'You know very well that's not what I meant. I want to take you out alone, without your two bodyguards.'

'They're not my bodyguards,' she scoffed.

'Really? So why, in that case, are their gazes riveted onto us?'

Kate swivelled her head, and sure enough both of her friends were intently watching her and Ross.

'See?' Ross whispered directly into her ear. His warm breath feathered the skin of her face, inducing a shiver all the way through her. She couldn't argue with him; he was right. But they hadn't just been looking; they'd also been listening, because Morwenna said, 'Pattie will babysit for you, Kate, if you want to go out.'

Kate glared at her so fiercely that Morwenna immediately fell silent. 'Traitor,' Kate hissed furiously.

'There you are,' Ross put in. 'You have no excuse now.'

And she was cornered, well and truly.

'So, shall we say tomorrow evening? I'll pick you up at seven thirty. I know a very good restaurant, not far from here, actually.'

It was at that point, with her two friends still all ears, that Kate surrendered to what was beginning to feel inevitable. With a sigh, she said, 'Okay.' *Get it over with*, she told herself. It would be a one-off occasion. Hopefully it would satisfy him, ensuring there'd be no need for a repeat performance.

Ross sat back in his seat and softly said, 'Finally — success.' With that, it was as if he relaxed; and with the arrival of a waiter, they all gave their orders for food as well as another couple of bottles of wine.

'Are you trying to get us drunk?'

Brenda fluttered her eyelids at Dan. Clearly she'd given up on capturing Ross's interest and was now concentrating every scrap of her efforts on Dan. Kate heard her ask him, 'So, are you already taken, or are you available?'

Dan gave a shout of laughter and said, 'I'm totally available. Single and fancy-free.'

'Well, there's a coincidence. Me, too,' Brenda murmured seductively. 'In which case, let the chase begin.'

'Oh, you won't have to chase very hard, sweetheart,' Dan softly told her. 'Not looking like you do.' His gaze lowered to the inches of cleavage on display.

Brenda turned her head slightly and winked mischievously at Kate, mouthing, 'My turn to score.'

'I'm beginning to feel very much the odd woman out here,' Morwenna sighed. 'The chaperone, in fact.' But she laughed with good humour. 'Good job I'm already spoken for.'

The rest of the evening progressed with a great deal of joking and merriment, the three bottles of wine taking their toll on all of them — except for Morwenna and Ross, who were both driving. As for Kate, the minute she tried to stand as they were preparing to leave, she lost her balance and sat straight down again, or tried to. The trouble was, she looked set to miss the chair completely and end up on the floor. Fortunately, Ross saw what was about to happen and managed to catch her. He then pulled her upright, and straight into his arms.

Kate was stunned by the sheer strength of her response to the feel of his arms around her, the thrill that stabbed at the pit of her stomach. But that was just for starters. Because when his head lowered to hers and his mouth brushed her parted lips, she all but stopped breathing altogether.

'Until tomorrow,' he murmured, gazing deep into her eyes. 'Seven thirty. Be ready.' He grinned down at her. 'Till then, goodnight.' And he kissed her again, for longer and with considerably more passion. This time Kate did actually stop breathing, as to her dismay she found herself kissing him back. He gathered her closer, letting her feel the hardness of his body, the strength of his desire. She gave a small gasp as he deepened the kiss. It was as if they were completely alone.

But then Dan said, with laughter in his voice, 'Okay, Ross, old man, put her down. The entire pub's watching, open-mouthed.'

Despite that, Ross took his time releasing her, his eyes smouldering and much darker than usual. They were the exact shade of treacle toffee. Kate couldn't mistake his arousal. Once again, an even more powerful thrill shot right through her as she felt her own body respond. Oh, good grief. What the hell had she done, agreeing to go out with him, just the two of them? If she felt this way after a mere kiss, where would she find the willpower to resist him if he tried to make love to her for real?

Kate stared at him, confusion filling her, before she turned to look at Dan. His eyes, in complete contrast to Ross's, were alight with mirth as he said, 'Time to go. It's not long to wait. Let's see ... ' He made a big performance of consulting his wristwatch. ' ... a mere twenty-one hours. Will you manage to wait that long, old man?' He was looking at Ross, his eyes still dancing. And Kate couldn't believe it when she heard Ross murmur back, his heated gaze still fixed on her, 'It'll be difficult, but I'll have to, won't I?'

As for Kate, she couldn't have spoken if her life depended on it. The strength of her emotions in response to his kisses had more than shaken her; they'd exploded within her, practically pulverising the very core of her, as had the feelings of loss she'd experienced when he taken his arms away from her. And of course, he knew that as well. The look on his face told her as much, more clearly than any words could have.

'Phew,' Brenda said as they walked back to Morwenna's car. 'Some kiss or what? The floor practically melted beneath you. I'm so envious. Mind you, I think Dan's interested. What do you two think?'

'It's a distinct possibility,' Morwenna replied.

'Kate? What do you think?' Brenda then asked.

'I think he was certainly interested in something. Your cleavage, maybe?' Kate lightly joked.

'Well, it's a beginning.' Brenda gave a loud laugh. 'I only want a bit of fun, so if he's up for that ... ' She shrugged her shoulders.

But Kate had retreated into her own confused world. She couldn't recall ever being quite so moved by a man's kiss before, not even Simon's. And Ross's had stirred something deep within her, something that left her distinctly unsettled yet desperately wanting more.

Brenda was still prattling on. 'Dan's good-looking, isn't he? Not as good-looking as Ross, of course; but clearly —' She slanted a glance in Kate's direction. '— he's taken.'

'Well and truly, I would've said,' Morwenna agreed, also directing a glance Kate's way.

'Still, I don't mind. I'm quite happy with Dan. You could drown in those forget-me-not eyes of his.'

The drive back to Bodruggan was accomplished in record time. They dropped a still-ecstatic Brenda off first and then went on to Honeysuckle Cottage.

Ellie and Matt were in bed, but Pattie and Imogen were glued to the television screen. 'Everything been all right?' Kate asked.

'Yeah,' Pattie told her, 'although the phone rang a couple of times. I answered it, but there was no reply.'

'That would be those damned computer-generated sales calls,' Morwenna said. 'They're a nuisance. It should be made illegal.'

And that was all it took. Unease renewed its grip on Kate. One thing she could be sure of, though — the calls, if they had been malicious rather than sales calls, couldn't have been made by Ross. He'd been at her side all evening. Not that she could imagine him doing such a thing, anyway. After this evening's events, she'd more or less discounted him being in any way connected to Robert Wilmot, let alone being the murderer.

But that aside, come next morning her worries returned, worsening her headache; the direct result, she conceded guiltily, of the amount of wine she'd consumed the evening before. She groaned. But far worse than that was the fact that she'd agreed to go out with Ross St. Clair. Whatever had possessed her? He wasn't her type at all, as she'd firmly declared on a couple of occasions now. Okay, his kisses had been pretty mind-blowing, but you needed more than mere kisses to cement or even begin a relationship. Maybe she could ring him and cancel ... except she didn't have his phone number. He'd be in the directory though, wouldn't he? She quickly checked, only to discover he wasn't. She should have expected that, a man of his wealth and success. He wouldn't want just any-old-body ringing him.

Her head began to thump even harder; agonisingly hard. In a bid to clear it, she piled the two children into the car along with a picnic basket and all their beach paraphernalia, and set off for one of the nearby beaches. Morwenna had told her about a small sandy cove just eight or nine miles away. So that was where she headed, with Ellie talking nonstop, and Matt worrying about whether she'd brought his armbands or not, despite her repeatedly insisting she had.

The day was a perfect one, with a sky so blue they could have believed they were in the Mediterranean rather than Cornwall. She easily located the beach and was relieved to find it empty. They spread the blanket she'd remembered to bring on the golden sand, and within a matter of minutes the children were in their bathing costumes, covered in suntan cream, and Kate was in her own costume. Buckets and spades were found and brought out, and in a very short time a truly splendid sand castle had been constructed, complete with a moat and corner turrets.

Kate relaxed back onto the blanket and abandoned herself to the hot sunshine.

Seagulls circled overhead, squawking and screeching noisily; but apart from that and the occasional sound of a motorboat engine, there was absolute silence. With their castle completed, both children were engrossed in adding a boat that they could both sit in. Peace reigned. Kate's eyes began to close.

'Mummy, can we go into the sea?' Ellie asked.

Kate sat up quickly and saw that the tide had come in. The sea was now lapping just feet away from her. 'Of course you can.' It would be safe this close to her. 'Keep hold of Matt's hand, though.'

She sat, alert as she watched her children playing, and decided that she had to put her fears and anxieties into some sort of perspective. She was becoming paranoid. No one was going to hurt her in this corner of the land. Not Ross, not anyone. He'd made no secret of his attraction to her, the way he looked at her told her how he felt. She'd stop worrying about every glimpse she thought she saw of someone turning a corner;

stop wondering whether every car that drove behind her was a threat; refuse to worry about the occasional silent phone call. Morwenna was right — they were nothing more threatening than sales calls. They happened all the time nowadays to everyone who owned a phone. She'd simply let herself enjoy the company of a handsome, incredibly sexy man. A man who was beginning to appear the exact opposite to the arrogant individual she'd initially believed him to be.

★ ★ ★

But come six thirty, her nervousness flooded back and yet again she found herself rifling through her wardrobe, wondering what to wear. She'd have to buy herself some new clothes. She worked in a flipping dress shop, after all, and Brenda had told her she'd get a good staff discount. But that didn't help her right at this moment.

In the end, she opted for a pair of white skinny trousers and a jade-green fitted tunic top, over which she slipped a lightweight taupe-coloured jacket. It wasn't quite the sophisticated designer look she'd have liked, but it would have to do. To compensate for any deficiencies in her outfit, she painstakingly applied her makeup, then brushed her hair till it shone, letting it cascade smoothly down onto her shoulders. Her skin had started to tan during her time on the beach and her nose and cheekbones had a rosy glow, even with the makeup she'd applied. She didn't need any blusher, that was for sure.

Pattie arrived in good time, which was just as well, because punctually at seven thirty Kate's doorbell chimed. Her heartbeat promptly leapt off the scale and every one of her anxieties flooded back. What the hell had she let herself in for? The truth was, after those amazing kisses the previous evening, anything could happen. Anything at all. Not least because she couldn't trust herself to resist the strong attraction that had overwhelmed her as Ross kissed her.

# 6

With her breath catching in her throat, Kate opened the door to see Ross standing there, looking devastatingly handsome and dressed to kill, making her feel even more drab and unimaginative. He wore an open-necked tan shirt teamed with a chocolate-brown immaculately tailored linen jacket and fawn trousers. It was a look that emphasised his already leonine qualities. Deliberate? she wondered. She wouldn't be surprised. She suspected he knew exactly how handsome he was, and, moreover, exactly how to emphasise that.

His gaze slid over her as he smiled and murmured, 'You look good enough to eat.'

She wasn't sure what to say to that, so opted for silence. It didn't stop her nerves from jangling wildly, however, as her heartbeat joined in with all the activity and raced, all because his words had instantly revived her fears as to what this evening would lead to. And this uncertainty wasn't in any way tempered as she met his gaze. He looked ... well, wolfish would be the most apt description. She swallowed as she spotted those intriguing and increasingly familiar gold flecks in his amber eyes. She still couldn't decide what it was they indicated, although judging by the way he'd looked at her in the bistro the evening before, she'd begun to think it could be desire.

'Shall we go?' he asked.

'Yes,' was all she was capable of saying. Honestly, she was beginning to sound as unexciting as her appearance suggested.

He led the way along the driveway towards the car parked at the kerbside. He hadn't brought the Range Rover. Again, Kate's breath caught in her throat, for Ross St. Clair was driving a black BMW, frighteningly similar to the car that had hounded her through the lanes. She swallowed as her nerves screamed. It couldn't have been him after all, could it? If it had, then here she was, going out to dinner with him, alone. What should she do? Confront him with her suspicion? Accuse him, even? Demand he tell her the truth?

But they'd reached the car before she could make her decision, and Ross was opening the front passenger door for her to get in. She hesitated and stared at him, her eyes, she was sure, blazing with uncertainty and — yes, fear.

'Kate?' he said, taking hold of her by the elbow. 'What is it? What's wrong? You're very pale. Do you feel ill?'

He did look genuinely concerned. Would he look like that if he was planning to harm her? Was she, once again, overreacting, seeing danger where there was none? The truth was, nothing he'd done up till now had suggested he was a threat to her. At least, not the sort she was now thinking of. In fact, it had been the very opposite. She recalled his offer of help should she ever need it. Mentally she shook herself. She was being silly. Both of her friends knew she was going out with him, so if anything should happen to her, Ross would be the first person to come under suspicion. And he'd know that. Whatever else he might be, he wasn't stupid.

She shook her head. 'No, I'm-I'm fine. A momentary dizziness, that's all.' She slipped into the front seat.

'Well,' he said with a smile, 'I don't usually have that effect on a woman. Should I take it as a compliment?'

She shrugged. 'I wouldn't. It's just tiredness. I didn't sleep well last night.'

His grin now was a rakish one, and she realised what it was she'd implied.

'I hope it wasn't thoughts of our meeting that kept you awake,' he murmured. 'I hesitate to call it a date, knowing your aversion to that particular description.'

He was being deliberately provocative now, she decided, and his subsequent grin confirmed that. 'Rest assured, it wasn't,' she sharply told him. The last thing she wanted was for him to assume she was in any way disturbed by thoughts of him. 'I've got one or two things on my mind, that's all. In fact, it was probably more to do with the wine I drank than anything else. I'm not usually much of a drinker.'

He strode around the car and joined her inside. 'Well, we'll have to make sure you don't overindulge this evening. I don't want to be responsible for your lack of sleep tonight as well, at least not from the after-effects of wine.' He slanted a glance at her as he turned the ignition key. 'I'd much rather that it was down to something more ... exciting than that.'

She knew instantly what he meant. A quiver of desire warned her of the peril she might be opening herself up to. Not the sort of peril that would harm her, but the sort of peril that allowing him to kiss her might lead to. For she genuinely didn't know whether she possessed the strength to resist him. She certainly hadn't done much of that the evening before.

It felt like mere moments to Kate before he was parking outside of a very classy-looking restaurant. Her heartbeat was still racing and her pulse leaping, both of which intensified as she wondered nervously whether she was dressed appropriately for such a place. She bit at her bottom lip. Maybe she should have worn the blue dress after all. It certainly looked the sort of place where the maître d' would frown at anyone attired in anything less than designer wear.

However, the formally dressed man who greeted them smiled warmly, immediately putting her at ease as he said, 'Good evening, Mr St. Clair. Madam. How are you both?' Clearly, the restaurant was a favourite haunt of Ross's.

'Good evening, Marco.'

'Please, I will show you to your table — or would you prefer a drink in the bar first?'

'We'll go straight to the table, I think.' Ross lifted a quizzical eyebrow at Kate, to which she murmured, 'That's fine by me.' At which point, her stomach gave an audible growl. Oh no. Not now; not here. She knew she flushed an unbecoming scarlet at such times, and she suspected that that was what was happening as she met Ross's grin of amusement.

'I think we'd better have the menu too, Marco. And could you bring a bottle of champagne? My usual, please.'

'Certainly, sir.' Marco turned and led the way to a table set for two in a private corner. It was laid up with a starched white cloth overlaid with one of rose pink; matching pink dinner serviettes; long-stemmed crystal wine glasses, two for each of them, as well as a water glass each; and heavily patterned silver cutlery. A chunky candle burned in the centre of an arrangement of scented pale lemon jonquil and white rosebuds. The whole effect was one of extreme and very tasteful luxury.

As she took her seat, Kate asked, 'What are we celebrating?'

'The fact that I've managed to get you to agree to come out with me.' Ross's expression was one of irritating satisfaction. 'I was beginning to think I'd never succeed. Are you always so difficult to persuade?'

'Not really.'

His gaze narrowed at her. 'So it was just me, then?'

That stumped her, because it *had* been

because of who he was; but she could hardly tell him that he had a disturbing likeness to a hardened murderer, and one who was at present languishing in a prison cell.

He quirked an eyebrow at her. Like Mags, it seemed to be a favourite trick of his, and one that Kate was pretty sure he knew enhanced his already startlingly good looks. It certainly didn't make him look ridiculously surprised, as it did her. But whereas Mags had employed it to indicate displeasure, on Ross it simply bestowed quizzical anticipation of whatever it was she intended to say. And, of course, that rendered her mute.

'Nothing to say?' The eyebrow rose even higher.

'No. Well, what I mean is, it wasn't just you. I haven't been out in an evening, not properly, for a long time.'

'You were out last evening, and you were at Morwenna's dinner party.'

'That was different. I meant I haven't been out with-with a ... '

'A man?' he finished for her. 'How

come, a lovely woman like you? You must have them practically queuing up.'

'I can assure you I don't.'

'You astonish me.'

'I-I simply haven't wanted to, not since my ...' She couldn't finish. Her throat filled up, just as it invariably did whenever she tried to mention Simon. She should be moving past this extreme reaction by now. It had been over twelve months since he died. And they hadn't really been that close for quite a while before that. Truth to tell, he'd been distant, detached even, for a few months prior to his death. They'd rarely made love, and hadn't spent that much time together. So, not altogether surprisingly — inevitably, in fact — she'd begun to wonder if he was having an affair. It would have explained his coolness towards her. But there'd never been any evidence of that. No unexplained expenditure, no scent of someone else's perfume on him when he eventually came home, no traces of lipstick on his shirts. She'd even on one occasion found herself, to her shame, going through his pockets and his wallet, but she'd found nothing apart from the usual receipts for petrol, car parking tickets, and restaurant bills for meals for one. None of it incriminating, and all perfectly acceptable.

But nonetheless, his increasing indifference towards her had suggested that there was something not right, and he had begun to travel more — on business, he'd told her. When she'd finally asked him what was wrong, and if he wasn't happy with her any longer, because they spent so much time apart, he'd regarded her as if she was mad and said, 'I'm busy. I rush about all day long. By the time I get home, I'm worn out. Life's tough out there at the moment. You have no idea,' he'd concluded scornfully.

And that had been that. She'd dropped the subject and they'd carried on as before, until he died in the car crash, and she was left wondering what had been the problem. There had been a couple of women at his funeral that she hadn't recognised. When she'd spoken to them, they'd each told her they were colleagues of Simon's, and as there'd been no indication of any sort of guilt, she'd decided to put her suspicions to rest. Simon was dead. None of it mattered anymore.

'Your husband died,' Ross gently finished for her. 'I heard you telling Mags. It must've been hard for you all.'

'It was.'

'You keep in touch with your family, presumably? That must be a comfort for you.'

'Simon had more or less lost touch with his parents, and he was an only child.' She shrugged. 'His mother left when he was ten and married an American, so she lives in the United States now. His father had already emigrated to Australia by the time I met Simon, and he's also remarried. So we don't have any contact with them, not even a Christmas card.'

'That's a shame.'

'Not really. As I said, I never knew them, and what the children have never had, they don't miss.'

He cocked his head and continued to

watch her, his expression sympathetic now. 'So you've come here, to Cornwall. To escape your memories? Your sadness?'

'Yes.' It seemed the easiest thing to say. She couldn't, after all, tell him the truth.

'A long way to come, isn't it?'

'I'd been here on holiday as a girl with my family and also a few times with Simon and the children. It seemed as good a place as any. Plus, it means the children will grow up in a peaceful and clean environment.'

'And how do Ellie and Matt feel about the move?'

That did surprise Kate — that he'd remembered their names. 'They weren't happy at first, but they're slowly adjusting, even Matt. They've made friends here.'

'Maybe we could all go out sometime? You, your children, and me and Cleo? Does that appeal?' His expression was an intent one. 'I'd like to get to know them properly.'

'Why?' she bluntly demanded.

Ross blinked at that, visibly

wrong-footed by the question. 'Why? Well ... ' He took some time to consider the matter before going on. 'I'd like to get to know you properly as well, not just your children. Does that surprise you?'

Heavy lids shuttered his thoughts, and any emotion he might be feeling, from her, which made her wonder just what he was trying to conceal. Was that all he was interested in, getting to know her better? Or could he have some other motive? A less than honourable motive; a dangerous motive, even?

But he was waiting for her answer, so deciding to be honest with him, she said, 'It does, yes. I would've thought there were plenty of women — women without the sort of ties I have — who'd be interested in seeing you on a regular basis.'

He shrugged, his broad shoulders moving easily beneath his jacket. Kate felt her heart lurch in her breast. He was a very fit man. She wondered if he had a gym in that mansion of his. According to Brenda, he had almost everything else.

'I'm sure there are,' he drawled. 'But none of them interest me, not like you do.'

That shook her. So much so, that she had no answer for him.

'Kate,' he sighed, 'you are a very lovely woman, but it's not just that. There are plenty of lovely women around. There's an air of — of vulnerability about you. It makes me want to take care of you.'

'I don't need taking care of,' she blurted, stung by the way he made her sound pathetic — helpless, even. And she wasn't, no matter what her fears and problems were. She'd had to be strong, for the sake of her children. 'Not by you, not by anyone,' she went on.

His face darkened, and he seemed about to retaliate just as hotly as she had to his remark, when a waiter appeared with a bottle of champagne — very expensive champagne, if Kate was any judge.

'Sir, shall I pour it?' He expertly popped the cork, and at Ross's nod, filled two flutes with skilled precision.

'Enjoy,' he then said before going again. Within another moment, a second waiter appeared and they gave their orders for dinner. By which time, Ross's expression had lightened again, and clearly deciding to let the sensitive topic of conversation go, he raised his glass to Kate and said, 'Here's to your good health and your and your children's happiness.'

She, too, raised her glass to him and murmured, 'Thank you.'

'Tell me about your family, Kate. I presume you have some, and that they're still in the midlands? Where, exactly?'

She blinked at him. 'Where —?'

'Yes. Where do they live?' He was frowning at her. He'd obviously picked up on her spasm of panic. No one, till now, had actually pinned her down on the place, so she hadn't been forced to give a detailed lie — something she wasn't very good at. People were, in general, very willing to simply accept something vague like the midlands.

'Uh — the same place I lived, a small town called Shrawton. Well, a village, really. You wouldn't know it.'

'No.'

'My mother's also widowed; my father died ten years ago — cancer. And I have one sister.'

'You must miss them.'

'I do, yes.'

'You're in touch with them, presumably?'

She hesitated, but when she saw his expression sharpen once more, with curiosity this time, she said, 'Yes, of course. But tell me about yourself.' She didn't want any more questions about her life or her family. It was far too sensitive a topic, and really, what could she tell him safely? But it was her deep-seated fear that she'd heedlessly blurt out something she shouldn't that made her steer the conversation away from herself and her family. However much she tried to reassure herself about Ross and his motives concerning her, she actually knew very little about him.

He readily accepted her change of tack and said, 'Well I'm divorced, as you know, and I have one daughter, Cleo. My parents live on the north coast, at a small place called Rock. It's not far from Padstow.'

'I know of it,' Kate murmured. 'I haven't visited yet, but I've heard about it.'

'I have a brother, younger than me, just married for the second time to a very nice woman called Stella. They don't have children. I live at Bodruggan House, again as you know. I bought it between four and five years ago, when Cleo decided she wanted to live with me — I think I explained that too.' He grinned at her.

'Yes, you did.' She returned his smile. 'But most girls opt to live with their mothers — well, most children do, boy or girl. I know she didn't like the idea of Scotland, but still, it's unusual. She'd have only been ... what, ten, eleven?'

'Ten — just.'

It must've been hard for you, too, coping with a ten-year-old girl? I know how difficult Ellie can be.'

'It *was* hard at times, but we got

through it. She had a nanny for two, almost three years before she decided she was too old for that.' He grinned ruefully. 'Which, I have to admit, she was. She's very mature for her age.'

'Yes,' Kate murmured. 'I could see that when you gave us a lift.'

'She can be a little ... forthright at times.'

Kate regarded him in silence for a moment or two, then asked, 'And you've never wanted to remarry?'

'I've never met anyone I could imagine spending the rest of my life with. I made a bad enough mistake the first time. I have no wish to repeat that.' His expression was a strange one then, leading Kate to wonder whether he still loved his wife, despite their problems.

'What do you do, businesswise?' she asked him, though she already knew a great deal about that, Brenda having filled her in. Still, it gave them something to talk about, and there was nothing like getting the facts from the horse's mouth.

'Oh, all sorts, really. Property

development, mainly in the world of leisure. I've got an interest in technology; custom-built websites for large businesses, for example. We also operate a couple of call centres for advice and aftercare. I set up all that up just three years ago. I deal on the stock market. It all keeps me busy.'

She couldn't resist asking then, 'Do you ever get up to the midlands?'

'Yes, quite often as a matter of fact. I do a lot of business in Birmingham.'

Kate felt the ground shift beneath her. So he could have been there at the time of the murder, and not in Australia as he'd told people. She decided to probe a little deeper. 'What were you doing in Australia?'

'Business — in Sydney mainly, then Melbourne for a while, and then across to Perth. I've got a substantial interest in a building project in Melbourne, and I'm setting up a couple of other things in Sydney and Perth — chiefly IT, the same sort of thing that I'm doing here in fact. Anyway, enough about me. I presume your family will visit you here. Maybe I can take you all out?'

Kate was stunned. What was happening here? Why was he so interested in her family? 'Well, there are no immediate plans for that.'

'Really?' He looked surprised. 'Don't Ellie and Matt miss their grandmother? Especially if she's the only grandparent they have.'

'Yes, but they understand it's not easy for her — the travelling, and my sister works.' Her words petered out.

'Couldn't you go there? I make regular trips up that way. I could easily give the three of you a lift.'

'No, please — it's not possible.'

Ross sat back in his seat, his long fingers playing with the stem of his glass as he studied her keenly. 'What's wrong, Kate? And don't say nothing, because it's all too obvious that there is something. Have you had a row?'

'Please.' She was almost pleading with him, but she couldn't stop herself. 'It-it's nothing like that. I just want the children to settle down here before we return. It will just resurrect … ' Again, she abruptly stopped talking. She'd been about to say too much, and confide her fears — just as she'd been afraid she would.

'What? What will it resurrect?'

'Old feelings. They miss their friends, and if I take them back … Please, just leave it.'

He stayed silent then, although his gaze didn't leave her. 'Okay,' he finally said, 'if that's what you want.'

'It is. Can we talk about something else?' If they didn't, she was genuinely terrified she'd reveal the truth; a part of it, anyway, about the real reason why they were here in Cornwall. The champagne had already begun to loosen her tongue, and she'd said more than she'd intended. But more than that, Ross's eyes had warmed as his gaze roamed over her, lingering far too long on her mouth — as if he were imagining kissing her again, as he had in the bistro last night. Even as she had the thought, her heart pounded and her pulse throbbed. She was in very dangerous territory. If he did begin to make love to her, she was almost sure she wouldn't have the strength to resist him. It had been too long since she'd made love with anyone, even Simon.

She was gratified, therefore, when he took his cue from her, and they began discussing everything from the food they liked to their favourite writers and the books they'd written. He told her more about his house, describing it in some detail.

'You'll have to visit,' he said, adding, 'I'm sure Cleo would like to meet you — again.'

Kate was quite sure she wouldn't. Cleo had made it obvious she resented Kate and her children's presence in the Range Rover the afternoon they had accepted her father's offer of a lift home. In fact, her attitude had seemed little short of contemptuous; certainly it had been scornful. Kate suspected that she was possessive of her father, viewing any other woman as a rival for his time and attention.

It wasn't until they were driving back to Bodruggan once again that Ross said, 'I want to see you again, Kate. I like you. I like you very much.'

Kate gazed at him through the darkness inside the car, her eyes wide, her lips parted. So much for her determination to avoid having to repeat this evening's outing. Ross, evidently, had other ideas. He turned his head and stared back at her, his eyes devouring her, quickening her pulse and setting her entire body aflame with desire.

She didn't need to put any of that into words. He instantly recognised her need, and before she could utter as much as a word, he'd pulled the car off the road into a convenient lay-by, where he turned the engine off and swivelled in his seat to look at her.

'But you know that, don't you?' His words were throaty, his smile a shaky one. 'Just as you know how much I want you.'

Kate couldn't speak, the ability seeming to have completely deserted her.

'Say something,' he murmured

hoarsely. 'You can't look at me like that and not.'

He reached across the car for her and roughly pulled her towards him. He encircled her with one arm, while with his free hand he cupped her chin and tilted her head backwards. With no hesitation at all, his mouth captured hers, his tongue forcing her lips apart to explore the sweet depths within.

All Kate could do then was respond. She slid her arms around his neck as somehow, despite the central console dividing their seats, he pulled her even closer. He moved his hand then, threading his fingers through the back of her hair, holding her in position as he deepened the kiss, grinding his mouth over hers. She heard him groan as he lowered his hand and brought it round to the front, sliding it down her arched throat to finally enclose her one breast with his fingers. As he began to gently caress her through the thin fabric of her tunic, she felt as if she were naked. His fingertips brushed her peak, arousing her desire to unbearable heights. She heard her own deep-throated groan. It had been so long …

'Come home with me — please. I want you so much.'

And that was all it took, that simple statement; and sanity rushed back to her. What on earth was she permitting him to do? She jerked away from him, while simultaneously pushing him back from her. 'No, I can't.'

The skin of his face paled dramatically. 'Why not? There's someone with the children, isn't there?'

'Of course; Pattie's there. But I can't simply not go home. Anyway, it wouldn't be right.'

He regarded her through eyes that were no more than slits; his mouth had compressed to a thin line. 'You'll need to explain that to me, I'm afraid. You're a woman, I'm a man. We clearly want each other. What's not right about that?'

'No.'

'No — what? You don't want me, too?' His scepticism was only too visible in the arching of his eyebrow, the glint in his eye. 'Excuse me if I don't believe you. The way you've just kissed me makes it only too obvious that you do.'

'I can't. I can't be with anyone.'

'Why not? Is there someone else? Is that it?'

'No. I just can't. I'm not ready — it's not the right time.'

He gave a low snort of disbelief. 'You seemed more than ready to me. Positively eager, in fact.' A grim smile now twisted his lips.

'I-I was c-carried away. I've been drinking.'

'I can't argue with that, but it wasn't just down to the effects of the alcohol, was it?'

She nodded. 'Yes, it was. I've never been able to drink much — as you witnessed last evening.'

'Okay. So when do you think you *will* be ready? Just so that I know.'

'I don't know. My life at the moment is …' What? she asked herself. What could she say? If she said it was extremely difficult, he'd almost certainly want to know what the problem was, and she couldn't tell him. Couldn't tell him that she was living a lie; couldn't expose her secret.

'Is what?' He was beginning to exhibit definite signs of impatience with her.

She had to say something, or he wasn't going to let the matter drop. 'I have two children who need me.'

'I know that, but they aren't going to lose you just because you start seeing me. And I'm sure they wouldn't want to deprive you of male companionship.'

'It's not just them.'

'Kate.' He sighed. He was definitely losing patience with her. 'If it's not just them, what is it?'

'It's not the right time; I've told you.'

He sighed. 'So you have. Okay.' He swung away from her and turned on the ignition. 'In that case, I'd better take you home.' He looked at her once more. 'But I meant what I said. I want to see you again, and if it's just friendship you want, that's okay — for now. But Kate, I won't wait forever.'

# 7

It was three o'clock in the morning when the phone by Kate's bed rang. She picked it up, only to find there was no one on the other end. She dialled 1471 but was told there was no number to return the call. It happened twice more, at four thirty and six o'clock precisely.

Her initial thought was, could it be Ross? But why he'd be calling in the early hours and then not responding, she couldn't imagine. And in any case, he didn't know her number, either her mobile or the landline, and the latter wasn't in the phone directory yet. Presumably she'd have to wait for the next edition; and even then, considering the position she was in, masquerading under a false name and living in what was technically a rented property, she was doubtful she'd be included.

She waited until nine o'clock and then

rang Bob Turpin. She told him what had happened, but he didn't sound overly concerned. She didn't mention the other incidents because she still wasn't sure that they didn't have perfectly innocent explanations.

'It's most likely one of those wretched call centres,' he said. 'I'm always getting them.'

'What, in the early hours of the morning? Is that likely?'

'Who knows what's likely these days? They don't seem to care what time it is.'

She ended the call. Bob was right; she was panicking over nothing. She'd received dozens of such calls in Birmingham, always when she was in the middle of something. Nevertheless, a feeling of unease niggled away at her as she recalled Pattie saying she'd also received a couple while she was babysitting.

In the end, Kate decided that she needed to get out of the house and be amongst people, her friends. Drive the whole thing from her mind. She could well be worrying needlessly. And, as it was

Sunday, Brenda would be free. She didn't open the shop on that day, declaring that she needed some free time. But when Kate spoke to her, Brenda joyfully told her, 'I'm meeting Dan.'

'Dan?'

'Yeah, you know — Ross's friend.'

'Oh, of course. That's great. Well, have a good time.'

'Don't worry about that,' Brenda chuckled. 'I intend to.'

She then rang Morwenna, but she was expecting Brett home at any moment. Which left Kate at a loose end. To make matters worse, both children were in serious whinge mode, especially Ellie. She complained over and over that she missed her gran and aunt — they'd more often than not gone to visit them on a Sunday — so they ended up packing a picnic once again and setting off for the beach.

After that, the days seemed to run swiftly, one into another. There was one reassuring thing, however — there were no more silent phone calls. Kate concluded that Bob had been right, and it had just been a call centre making a nuisance of itself.

Gradually she forgot about it, at the same time wishing she could do the same with regards to Ross. He hadn't been in touch, so she could only assume he'd had second thoughts about her, maybe accepting that she genuinely wasn't ready for any sort of relationship, and had decided to abandon the chase. She should have felt relieved, but paradoxically she felt nothing of the sort. Images of him with another woman constantly presented themselves to her mind's eye, inflicting a kind of torment upon her: an aching longing to feel his arms around her and his mouth on hers, and no matter how hard she tried she couldn't make it go away.

Then, out of the blue, a letter arrived. It must have been hand-delivered, because it just had her name, printed in capital letters, on the envelope. No address; no stamp. With a growing sense of unease — it felt scarily similar to the anonymous phone calls — she opened it and pulled out the single sheet of notepaper that was folded inside. She read:

KEEP YOUR MOUTH SHUT OR YOU'LL REGRET IT.

That was all. There was no signature; and the words, like her name on the envelope, were printed in capitals. She read them again, and then a third time, with a heart that was pounding and a stomach that churned with panic and fear.

She then opened the front door and gingerly poked her head out. Quickly she glanced around. There was no one to be seen; whoever had brought this had gone.

Her mind raced in crazy circles. There was only one conclusion she could logically draw. Robert Wilmot knew where she was. Or one of his partners in crime did, because, after all, he was safely locked up. And this letter made it abundantly clear that they were determined to silence her.

She had her hand on the phone to call Bob when something stopped her. *Think about this*, she cautioned herself. *Think hard. What would Bob do?* He'd most likely inform his superiors in the witness protection scheme, and what then? What if they wanted to move her somewhere else; insisted on it? She and the children would have to start over again. They'd have to leave the friends they'd all made, there'd be a new school ... She could already hear their protests, especially from Ellie: *I'm not going. You can't make me.* She'd glower fiercely and cross her arms over her chest, the very picture of defiance and rebellion. Kate had seen it all before.

She sighed. For the third — or was it the fourth? — time, she reread the words. They didn't actually threaten to physically harm any of them; just said that she'd regret it if she talked about the murder — in the courtroom when giving her evidence, presumably? And that could be months away; a year, even. This was simply scare tactics.

Well, she wasn't going to give in to them. She'd bide her time. Remain vigilant and on her guard. Keep a very close watch on the children. They mustn't go anywhere alone, but they didn't anyway. So no change there. She then ripped up the sheet of paper and the envelope it had come in into small pieces and buried them beneath the other rubbish in the bin.

As it was Thursday morning, she needed to get the children to school and herself to work. She'd drive. There'd be no more walking; that way they'd be less vulnerable. At least, she hoped so. But her heart sank as she recalled the feeling of being followed around town; the brief glimpses she'd caught of a man's back; the car behind her in the lane. Then there was the wreath that had been delivered, the silent phone calls, and now the anonymous letter. Could these things all be down to the same man? It was beginning to seem highly probable.

She agonised then, long and hard, over her decision to do nothing. Was she right to not tell Bob? Was she putting their happiness over their safety? Oh God, what should she do? If only she had someone she could confide in, someone to advise her. It couldn't be Bob, that was for sure. Even though he'd swiftly dismissed her worries about the phone calls, she doubted he'd dismiss all the other things as easily. And that meant the consequences could prove serious for her and her children. Disastrous, even.

By the time she arrived at work, Kate was a mass of indecision and deep, nagging anxiety. So much so that she was tempted to confide in Brenda. But her boss, as she had already decided once before, simply couldn't be relied on not to spread the information that her friend and employee was in hiding from a vicious killer. And if that news got round, as well as Kate's true identity — and if, as a result of that, a national newspaper picked up the story, which under the circumstances was more than possible; inevitable, even — then she'd have no option but to move. And the truth was, she simply couldn't face it. She buried the notion that, most of all, she wouldn't be able to bear leaving Ross.

* ★ *

It was nine o'clock on Saturday morning when her landline phone rang. Her nerves, which were already pretty well shredded, now fractured into pieces, staying her hand to leave her staring at it instead. Would this be another silent call? Or would it be a verbal threat? What if whoever had been behind the letter as well as the other disturbing incidents had decided to up their game? Till now, there'd been no definite threat to her. Even the delivery of the wreath could have been a simple mistake. It had all been no more than suspicion on her part about what was happening. A feeling of someone watching, following her; an instinct.

With her thoughts tumbling over themselves as she struggled to consider all options, she finally braced herself to pick up the receiver. 'H-hello,' she tentatively said.

'Kate — is that you?'

It was Ross. Relief flooded over her,

only for apprehension to instantly replace it. What did he want? 'Yes.' Her voice noticeably quivered. Just as her hand did.

'It doesn't sound like you. Are you not well?'

'I'm fine. The phone ringing just startled me, that's all. I didn't realise you knew my phone number.'

'I rang Morwenna and she gave it to me. She also gave me your mobile number. I hope you don't mind?'

'It's a bit late to mind now.' Even she could hear how terse she sounded. But, really, Morwenna should have asked her first.

'I suppose it is.'

She could hear the amusement in his tone, and her exasperation with him rose.

'How do you fancy a walk? You, Ellie, Matt, me and Cleo? We could drive to the Roseland peninsula. There are some very scenic walks there. I could bring a picnic. It's going to be a lovely day, apparently.'

Her heart leapt, banishing her exasperation with him in one swipe. She glanced through the window and saw what she hadn't noticed till then, so absorbed in her own concerns had she been — that it was indeed a glorious morning. The sky was the colour of periwinkle flowers. It was freckled with puffball clouds, and there was barely a breeze; the tops of the trees, bearing witness to this, were perfectly still. And she had to confess, the invitation was very tempting. It would get her and the children out of the house, if nothing else, and away from the possibility of any sort of disturbing incident occurring. That fact alone went some way to persuading her to agree. After all, what could happen between them if their children were present?

'Well, I fancy it,' she told him, 'but I'm not sure whether the children will.'

The children, however, instantly and gleefully agreed. 'As long as the walk's not miles and miles,' was Ellie's main condition. 'Because I don't think Matt's little legs would cope.'

Kate smiled to herself. As provisos went, that was a humdinger, because of course what Ellie meant was that her legs wouldn't cope.

Kate turned back to the phone. 'Okay, you're on.' She told Ross. 'We're all agreed.'

'Great.' And he did sound inordinately gratified, something that instantly cheered her. Maybe all wasn't lost, after all. Maybe they could have some sort of relationship ... but deep down, she knew that wasn't really possible. Ross was a passionate man, she knew that beyond any doubt. He wouldn't wait indefinitely; he'd made that transparently clear. He wanted a full-on love affair, and she didn't know if that would ever be possible. Nevertheless, she decided she'd enjoy today, in the company of a handsome man; a man who made no secret of the fact that he was attracted to her and physically wanted her — which, after Simon's hurtful coldness, was immensely reassuring. She must still have her sex appeal, she assured herself with a broad grin. So she'd put her worries about the future to one side — for now, at least, as she was pretty sure they'd return the moment she was alone again.

'I'll collect you all at ten thirty or there-abouts,' Ross was saying. 'I don't plan to be any later, but teenage girls can take ages to get ready.'

'Fine. We'll see you then — or about then.'

Kate smiled as she replaced the receiver on its base unit, recalling her own teenage days and her mother impatiently calling to her, 'Kate, how much longer are you going to be? For heaven's sake, we're only going shopping, not visiting the Queen.'

By the time ten o'clock arrived, both children were dressed and raring to go. Ellie was wearing a pair of hot-pink shorts and a matching pink and white striped T-shirt. Matt was in tan shorts and a white T-shirt, which Kate didn't expect to stay clean for very long, but the little boy had insisted. As for Kate, in the anticipation of a hot day she had slipped on a pair of mid-thigh cream shorts and a strappy turquoise top. She lathered them all with a high-factor sun cream and took sun hats for each of them. Ellie insisted on a bucket and spade for Matt, though she considered herself too old for such childish things. She did, however, include an inflatable beach ball — just in case, she told her mother.

'I think Cleo might be a little old for ball games,' Kate told her with a frown. She was remembering Cleo's disdain for them all. She simply couldn't imagine the teenager running around playing catch.

'I bet she isn't,' Ellie confidently predicted. 'Should I take my kite, Mum?'

'We'll see what Ross thinks,' Kate told her. 'It is a bit big.'

At exactly ten thirty, the Range Rover that they'd ridden in that first time appeared and parked at the kerbside in front of the cottage. The two children ran out to it, whooping with excitement.

Ross climbed from the driving seat and caught Matt as the little boy ran to him, tossing him into the air, to Matt's rapturous delight. Ellie, who believed herself far too old for such antics, walked serenely towards Ross, a superior smile decorating her pretty face.

Ross put Matt down and held out his hand to Ellie. He'd read her attitude exactly right, Kate acknowledged. That must be the result of living with a teenage girl. 'I must say, Ellie, you look rather lovely today. The colour definitely suits you.'

'Thank you,' Ellie said politely, and shyly added, 'You look very handsome, too.'

Kate had to agree. Like her, he'd put on a pair of cream shorts and a dark burgundy T-shirt. He had a cream sweater slung carelessly around his shoulders.

'Kate,' he said, finally turning to her. The sort of glance she was becoming accustomed to swept over her, and she watched as his eyes blazed with admiration. 'I have to say, I'm going to be the envy of every man we pass with three such lovely women as my companions. Cleo,' he called over his shoulder. The girl had remained in the front passenger seat, obviously staking her claim, Kate decided. She didn't mind; she'd happily sit in the back with her children. 'Come out and meet everyone.' There was the merest hint of reproof in his tone as his daughter continued to fiddle with her phone. Kate saw her mouth tighten with irritation, but then she climbed out to join the group on the pavement.

'Hello, Cleo,' Kate greeted her. 'You've met Ellie and Matt.'

'Obviously,' came the terse response. 'We gave you a lift the other day.'

'That's enough, Cleo,' Ross softly reprimanded her. 'Right, now — what's for the boot?'

'Can we bring the kite?' Ellie eagerly asked, her stiffly polite manner vanishing in an instant.

'You sure can.' Ross grinned. 'I've always loved flying a kite, and there should be enough of a breeze on the coast.'

Cleo merely raised an eyebrow at this childish display, but she refrained from comment.

'I've brought a few things as well.' Kate offered him her basket, which contained a few treats; things like fruit sweets, crisps, and lemonade for Ellie and Matt. There were some homemade biscuits and some cupcakes, which, luckily, she'd made the evening before in a fairly futile attempt to keep herself busy and so push all thoughts about Ross to the back of her mind.

'You didn't need to do that,' Ross said with an admiring grin. 'Mrs Elliot — Beth — has prepared us a feast. But thank you just the same. It all looks delicious.'

Aah. Kate had wondered who'd prepare the picnic. She should have guessed it would be the housekeeper. Ross didn't look like the sort of man to embark upon any sort of food preparation himself.

'Okay then.' He slammed the rear door closed. 'Everybody into the back, and we'll get going.'

They all climbed into their rear seats — even Cleo, though Kate could sense the waves of discontent radiating from the girl. Matt said, 'I'm not sitting in the middle,' to which Ellie replied, 'I'll sit in the middle, next to Cleo.'

Cleo didn't utter a word. She probably felt it beneath her dignity to participate in such a childish argument. It was probably bad enough, in her opinion, being relegated to the rear with the children.

'Everybody strapped in?' Ross called.

'Ye-es,' Matt and Ellie sang out.

'Cleo?' he then asked.

'Naturally. I don't need to be told to belt up.'

Which provoked hilarious laughter from Matt. 'Belt up, Cleo,' he shouted. 'Just belt up.'

'Matt,' Kate said, turning round to frown at her son, 'that's very rude. Say sorry — now.'

Matt hung his head and muttered, 'Sorree, Cleo.'

Ross was grinning broadly by this time. 'Right then, off we go.' Cleo hadn't uttered a word.

★ ★ ★

They reached the peninsula in record time, whereupon Ross parked the car and they all climbed out. 'Now what I thought we'd do,' he announced, 'is have our walk

165

and then return to the car, and I'll drive
to a nearby beach — well, a small cove
really — and we'll have our picnic there.
It's always quiet. I don't think anyone
knows about it, other than me of course.
That way we won't need to haul the hamper and all the other things along with us.
Kate, is that okay with you?'

'I'm totally in your hands,' she impet-
uously said, only to regret the words a
second later when Ross murmured, 'If
only,' before giving her the sexiest smile
she'd ever seen. It took her breath clear
away. As a result, her face flamed and
she didn't know which way to look, especially when she glimpsed unmistakable
condemnation in Cleo's eyes as the girl
stared at her.

Kate was horrified. Had she heard
her father's remark? It certainly looked
that way. And there'd been no mistaking
Ross's meaning. He wanted to hold her,
make love to her, and it was abundantly
clear that Cleo loathed the idea.

Belatedly aware that Ross was keenly
studying her flushed cheeks, she swung

away from him, asking lightly — well, as lightly as she could, given that her pulse was throbbing and she was only just regaining the power to breathe normally — 'Which way?'

A small smile was now flirting with the corners of his mouth, she noted when she dared a sideways peek at him. 'Straight ahead,' he said. 'Out of the car park and then left. Okay, kids, here we go. We'll leave the kite and everything else until we get to the beach.'

'I've brought a beach ball as well,' Ellie told him.

'Oh, goodie,' Cleo sarcastically remarked. 'What a treat.'

Kate sighed softly to herself as she strode out ahead of them all. They shouldn't have come. Thankfully, her two children remained sublimely unaware of Cleo's hostility towards them. It wouldn't take Ellie long to notice it, though, as she was acutely sensitive to other people's feelings; and once that happened, she wouldn't take kindly to her companion's acerbic comments. And she could be equally outspoken herself, which more or less guaranteed the row that would sooner or later erupt.

Ross caught up with her, and putting his arm around her shoulders, quietly said, 'Give her time. She's had me to herself for quite a while now, and she's clearly viewing you as serious competition.'

Kate regarded him and asked, her tone an accusing one, 'Why's that? What have you said to her about me?'

'Nothing much, but she's not stupid. She can see how attracted I am to you.'

'Is she hoping you and her mother will get back together?'

'No, I don't think so. Her mother's married again, as I told you the other evening. She's accepted that. It's me she's possessive of.'

'But you must have had girlfriends before?'

'Of course, but she senses something different this time.'

'Different?' Kate couldn't resist asking.

'Completely. You must have realised

when we went out together how I feel. That I want you — very, very much.' He murmured the last few words directly into her ear, his warm breath fanning her face, gently moving the wisps of hair that were hanging down. She shivered, a thrill quivering right through her.

Kate was still looking at him, and now she saw the way his eyes were smouldering as the familiar gold flecks appeared for the first time that day. His lips were close enough to hers now to kiss her. The breath caught in her throat, making her gasp and draw away.

'Kate,' he throatily murmured, 'please don't push me away.'

'Dad,' Cleo called from behind them, her irritation plain to hear, 'can you come back and walk with us? I'm not the bloody child minder.'

'Cleo!' Ross turned his head and spoke sharply. 'Mind your language, please.'

'Oh, don't worry, Mr St. Clair,' Ellie smoothly put in. 'We've heard swear words before.'

'Have you, now? And, please, it's Ross.

I hate being called Mr St. Clair. It makes me feel so old.' He grinned at the little girl. 'So tell me, where have you heard swear words? Not from your mother, I'm sure. She's far too much of a lady.'

'A lady?' Ellie snorted. 'You want to hear her sometimes when she's really, really cross.'

Kate turned now, as well, to glare at her daughter. 'Will you stop that — right now.'

'Well, you do swear,' Ellie indignantly went on. 'I've heard you. 'Oh God' — you say that all the time. 'That damned thing' — that's another favourite. 'Damn and blast it. Sh — ' '

'Ellie,' Kate burst out, 'stop. That's more than enough, thank you.'

Ross was practically helpless with laughter by this time, and even Cleo was cracking a smile. She said, 'I don't think that's considered real swearing, Ellie. Now if she'd said something like fu — '

Ross abruptly stopped laughing and glared threateningly at his daughter. 'Cleo, that's not funny.'

'Sorry, Dad.' But she slanted a grin at Ellie, making them both race ahead, well out of reach of their frowning parents, giggling so hard they had to stop running at one juncture and bend double as they gave way totally to their mirth. Matt trailed behind them, perfectly happy, talking to himself. 'What's 'fu' mean?'

As for Kate, all she could feel was relief. The ice had been broken, and they were all getting along famously. All right, it had taken a swear word or two, but who cared?

'So,' Ross drawled, slanting a teasing glance at her, 'you swear, do you? Somehow I can't imagine that.' His handsome features were wreathed in a smile. 'And the s-word, to boot. I'm shocked. You've seemed such a lady till now.'

She rolled her eyes at him. 'Yeah, right. I have been known to use it very, very occasionally. Doesn't everyone swear at times?'

'Of course, but your choice of words — on the whole ... ' He grinned at her, sending her pulse wild. ' ... is very mild.

You should hear some of the women I've known.'

'Oh? Do tell.'

'Not on your life. Suffice it to say, not one of them lasted more than a week, one in particular not even that. She'd have out-sworn pretty well most of the men I know. And on my travels, I've met a few … rough diamonds, shall we call them?'

She eyed him. 'What sort of company do you mix in?'

'All sorts, believe me. You can't help it when you get about as much as I do.'

'I see.' She paused, to add more impact to her next question. 'But it does sound as if you're not really a stayer.'

'Stayer?' He lifted an eyebrow at her.

'Yeah — as regards girlfriends, lovers, whatever.' She shrugged. 'They evidently don't last long. What was the longest? A week?'

'Oh, I see.' He cocked his head and regarded her, his stare a level one. 'Well, I'm hoping to go a bit longer this time — a lifetime, in fact,' he added, so softly she barely heard him.

'This time?'

'This time.' He stopped walking to pull her closer, at the same time glancing ahead to ensure the children weren't watching or listening. 'This time I want it to go on and on.' And he bent his head, letting his mouth gently rest on hers.

# 8

Kate couldn't help herself; her response was instantaneous. She parted her lips to him as her heart gave an almighty leap.

'Oh Kate,' Ross huskily murmured against her mouth.

She pulled back just a couple of inches and looked up at him from beneath lowered lashes. It was a provocative gesture, inducing a slow, deliberately sensuous smile from him and the soft question, 'Are you flirting with me? Because if you are, such behaviour could end up with me carrying you off, and ... ' He, too, now pulled away, provoking a sensation of unutterable disappointment from Kate. 'The kids are turning round.'

He must have kept an eye on the three of them throughout their kiss. Did that mean his heart hadn't been in it?

Of course, he detected her thoughts instantly. 'Don't look like that — please.

Just because I'm careful in front of the children doesn't mean my emotions weren't every bit as engaged as yours were.'

Kate had never known a man so attuned to other people's emotions. It made her feel vulnerable, incapable of protecting herself and her innermost thoughts from him. It also made her wonder how many women he'd been intimate with in order to be so knowledgeable about them and their emotions. That question sobered her up.

'Come on, Dad,' Cleo called. 'Are we walking or not?'

Ross took Kate's hand in his, murmuring, 'Once we're alone, well ...'

Passion and a deep, burning desire smouldered inside Kate, and her body once again instantly responded, as she admitted finally that she wanted him every bit as much as he wanted her, and to hell with everything else. Why shouldn't she embark upon a love affair? Indulge herself a little? She was single again, just as Ross was. Why should anything else matter?

She was still a young woman, with a life to live. She should do just that; live it.

With that decision made, her spirits lifted and she quickened her pace as they joined the impatient children and began their walk along the truly beautiful stretch of cliff-top path. The views were breathtaking — almost as breathtaking as Ross's kiss had been; and she smiled to herself, confident there was more of the same to come. She sighed then as a feeling of complete bliss swamped her.

'That was a big sigh,' Ross said. 'Are you okay?'

'I'm fine; just fine. This is wonderful. Thank you for bringing us.'

'That's okay. It's my pleasure, believe me.' He gave her the sort of smile that made her whole body burn and tingle, heightening every single nerve ending into a sensitivity that was almost painful.

Kate moved her gaze away from him. If he went on looking at her like that, she'd be throwing herself at him and pleading for him to hold her; to make love to her. In an almighty effort to distract herself from her increasingly desperate need to feel his arms around her and his mouth on hers, she looked out to sea; a sea that was so blue that it merged with the sky on the far horizon, making it impossible to tell where one ended and the other began. And yet she remained acutely aware of Ross watching her, a small smile yet again tilting the corners of his mouth and provoking a flush of pink to colour her cheeks. Which ensured that when the three children embarked upon a game of spotting and then naming the birds that flew all around them, relief swamped her. She had no wish to embarrass herself by making her desire for his lovemaking obvious — though she had a strong suspicion that he knew anyway.

'Herring gulls.' Ellie proudly pointed to the flock of birds that practically engulfed a small fishing boat sailing in with its catch. But it wasn't only sea birds that they could see. Jackdaws landed all around them as they walked, busily chattering between themselves. Swallows and swifts dived and swooped, and several members of the tit family joined in with the fun. They even saw a cormorant diving for fish before it flew off, skimming low over the millpond-calm water. There were mallard ducks with swans elegantly gliding amongst them, their cygnets following in a straight line behind. And beyond all of this were a dozen or so yachts, their gleaming white sails filled with the wind that was now blowing as they tacked back and forth across the bay. It was magical.

Eventually they decided they'd walked far enough and headed back to the car. It was then only a short drive along narrow lanes to the beach. The high hedges were liberally freckled with bluebells, clusters of primroses, bright yellow celandines and, lording it amongst them all, tall spikes of brilliant pink campions.

'I'm starving,' Matt suddenly informed them all.

'You would be,' Ellie loftily told him. 'When aren't you hungry?'

'Well, I'm a growing lad, aren't I, Mummy?'

'You are, my darling,' Kate fondly responded. It was Matt's one great disappointment, that he wasn't taller. He longed to be as tall as Ellie, who towered a good six inches above him. He was a small boy, it was true, but Kate wasn't worried. She'd been small at his age and a year or two later had suddenly shot upwards, seeming to grow a bit more every day. She suspected Matt would do the same.

And then, all of a sudden, they spotted the beach beneath them. They wound their way down a steeply sloping lane thickly overhung by tall beech trees; this created the impression of driving through a green tunnel, despite the rays of sun penetrating the dense foliage in places to provide a lacework of brightness and shadows on the surface of the road.

Ross parked the car not far from where they eventually sat. As he had told them, it was a small cove, and they were the only people there. The children spread the rug that he had thoughtfully brought along, and they all sat down with sighs of contentment.

He then opened the hamper and began to take out the food. Kate gasped at the feast that was spread out before them. There was a huge quiche, already sliced into five equal portions; an equally large bowl of salad leaves; small plum tomatoes; a sliced whole ham, already cut up; French bread; and a bowl of butter. There was also a selection of cheeses, fresh peaches, strawberries and raspberries, plus a substantial tub of cream — Cornish, of course. Plates and bowls also were brought out, along with silver cutlery and linen serviettes. As for drinks, there was a bottle of wine and two glasses for Kate and Ross, and a choice of lemonade or orange juice for the children.

It didn't take long for them to devour every last morsel, and then Kate brought out the biscuits and cupcakes and they ate most of those as well. When they'd finished eating, Ross and Kate lay back on the rug, while Matt and Ellie wanted to fly the kite while there was still a breeze. But Ross had groaned, 'Can't it wait? I'm too well fed to move a muscle,' inspiring

Cleo to say, 'I'll go with them. You two oldies have a rest.'

Kate, while previously merely surprised at the transformation in the teenager, now experienced deep gratitude to her. But the fact was, she appeared to be growing genuinely fond of the younger two. Maybe she just wanted her father to be happy, but after a series of bad choices of girlfriends by Ross had become wary and suspicious of everyone. Maybe Ross had been right, and she sensed something different about Kate. That thought filled her with happiness as, propped up on one elbow, she watched the three children run along the shoreline, Cleo dragging the kite behind her, letting the wind fill it and raise it high above their heads. Ellie and Matt gave a loud cheer, and even Cleo whooped with delight.

Kate sat up and lifted her glass to her lips to drain the last few drops of wine. She looked down at Ross lying alongside her, his eyes closed. She decided he was asleep and smiled down on him. But then, unexpectedly, he opened his eyes and stared straight up at her. For a second or two, he said nothing; he simply looked at her, eyes half-closed, his expression unreadable. Kate was hit by a belated feeling of doubt, as she wondered if she'd misinterpreted the signals she'd believed he was sending out to her, even his words of desire. Could he have been deliberately and cruelly misleading her, simply to have sex with her? After all, it wouldn't be the first time a man had done such a thing. But then his gaze warmed and he huskily murmured, 'Come here,' and she knew everything was all right.

Kate didn't argue. A swift sideways glance told her the children were a distance away and still happily engrossed in the flying of their kite, and thus were taking absolutely no notice of what their parents were doing. She lowered herself into his open arms, and when they folded around her she nestled into his side, tucking her head into the hollow between his chin and his shoulder.

But he wasn't having any of that. With an index finger he lifted her chin, tilting her head backwards, before he shifted so that he was facing her. The look on his face melted her inside. He pulled her closer, removing his hand from beneath her chin to cup the back of her head, placing her in the perfect position for his kiss.

'Oh, Kate,' he breathed, 'just the sight of you ... ' He began to thread his fingers through her hair, pulling a few strands towards him and burying his face into them. He gave a soft sigh of pleasure. 'You even smell wonderful. Do you have any idea at all what you do to me?'

'I'm beginning to,' she whispered back.

He didn't give her time to say anything else. Instead, he moved his head sideways to capture her mouth with his. Kate made no move to stop him. Instead, she pressed her body to his, letting him feel every inch of her. She wanted this every bit as much as he did. For the truth was that she was falling in love with him; deeply, madly, passionately. And there was nothing she could do to prevent it.

They stayed that way for several minutes, their kisses growing deeper and more passionate by the second. It was only the sounds of the children returning that forced them apart once more, and they both sat up, their breathing fast and, in Kate's case, her entire insides quivering with frustrated passion.

'Who wants a game with the beach ball?' Ellie asked as she began to inflate the plastic ball.

'We do,' Matt and Cleo shouted in perfect unison.

'Come on, Mum,' Ellie told her, 'a bit of exercise will do you good.'

The five of them ended up racing across the sand, throwing the ball to each other; that was, when their laughter allowed them to. Ross wholeheartedly joined in. In fact, Kate mused, he was being wonderful with Ellie and Matt, and understandably they loved it. Since Simon died, there hadn't been a man in their lives, and they'd missed that, especially Matt.

Eventually, happy and utterly weary, they piled back into the Range Rover and headed back to Bodruggan. Ross then quietly asked, 'Can you and I go out this evening? It would make for a perfect ending to what's been a perfect day.'

Kate, startled, stared at him. 'Um — well, not really. I can't just leave the children.'

He swivelled his head to look at Cleo and asked, 'Cleo, could you babysit for Kate this evening?'

'No can do, Dad. Have you forgotten? Mel's coming for a sleepover.'

'Oh — yes, of course she is.' He stared through the windscreen, his brow drawn down in a frown, before he turned to Kate and unexpectedly suggested, 'I could drop Cleo off and come back to yours.'

He looked — and sounded — nervous. Kate was taken aback. That was the very last thing she would have anticipated. She hadn't thought he had a nervous bone in his body. He always seemed so sure of himself — so confident; so self-possessed. Irritatingly so, on occasion. But now his demeanour had her questioning that assumption. Maybe she'd been wrong about him. Maybe he was human after all, like the rest of them, with all the normal anxieties and uncertainties. Maybe it was simply a front he put on in order to bestow the impression of the confidence, skill and efficiency he needed when conducting his day-to-day business. He wouldn't have been so successful, and accumulated so much wealth, otherwise. So maybe it wasn't surprising that that behaviour carried through into his personal life.

'Yeah, yeah,' Ellie and Matt cheered from the back seat. 'We could get fish and chips for supper.'

Kate couldn't help but grin at this. 'Did you three plan this together?' she asked Ross.

'No, honest.' He looked and sounded almost boyish. He glanced back at the children, his expression conspiratorial. They loved it, both chiming, 'No, honest, Mum, we didn't.'

'Hmmm,' was all she said, playing their game along with them.

'So what do you think?' Ross persisted

'Please, Mum,' Matt pleaded. 'We've had such fun today. I don't want it to end.'

'Neither do I,' Ellie added for good measure.

'But will Cleo and her friend be okay on their own?' Kate asked, deciding someone should be acting responsibly.

'Beth's there. She lives in. She'll keep an eye on things.'

After that, there didn't seem any reason to refuse. 'Okay then,' Kate said.

They dropped Cleo off at Bodruggan House. 'Bye, kids,' she said, waving to them. 'It's been good fun. We'll have to do it again. Bye, Kate.'

'Bye, Cleo,' they all chimed.

'Yes, we'll definitely do it again,' Ellie added. 'I can't wait.' Her broad smile assured Kate that she meant it. With that, a sensation of utter contentment engulfed her. For the truth was, she couldn't wait either.

Ross had parked the car on the front driveway — a vast circular, gravelled affair — before escorting Cleo inside.

Kate now looked around, her initial impression one of extreme wealth and good taste. The house itself, as Brenda had told her, was enviably large, three storeys high, and constructed in blocks of Cornish granite. It had a steeply sloping grey slate roof, which was topped with a regiment of ornamental chimney pots. Stone-mullioned windows, criss-crossed with diamond-shaped leaded lights, stretched across the front of the building. She counted seventeen in varying sizes, some clearly the height of the room inside, others ranging from normal window size to so small they barely counted as windows at all. A shallow flight of stone steps led up to a pair of double oak doors.

'Wow!' Ellie cried. 'It's huge! Does Ross live here on his own?'

'Not quite alone,' Kate told her. 'Cleo is here with him, and also quite a few members of staff I would think, judging by the size of it.'

Kate glanced away from the house to take in the immaculately mown lawns stretching away on each side of the long driveway as far as she could see. The area had been skilfully landscaped with large clusters of trees, mainly horse chestnut and beech she thought, but also with large beds of what looked like dozens and dozens of herbaceous plants. There was also a stable block, partially concealed by a high hedgerow. She couldn't see any horses, but she could certainly hear their gentle snickers and the clatter of their hooves on what was evidently stony ground.

She had no time to see any more as Ross returned and wasted no time at all in heading back to Honeysuckle Cottage via the chip shop in the town. The four of them then sat in front of the television and ate their meals out of the papers they had been served in, after which Kate said, 'Right, you two. Upstairs and brush your teeth.'

'Oh Mum,' Matt wailed predictably; Kate hadn't expected to get away with that so easily. 'Can't we stay up just for a while? It's Sunday tomorrow. We can lie in.'

'Okay. Do your bathroom chores, undress, and then come back down, but it's just for a little while.'

They raced each other up the stairs, creating enough noise to make it sound as if a pack of wildebeests had taken up residence. Kate sighed and gave a wry grin. 'Is Cleo this noisy? I suppose she's too old now.'

'Oh believe me, when she has friends staying over it's more or less the same. Now, another glass of wine?' He'd swiftly collected another bottle from his kitchen when they'd dropped Cleo off.

'Are you trying to get me drunk? We emptied the bottle at lunchtime.'

He sent her a look of guileless innocence. 'Now, why would you think I'd do such a thing?'

'I daren't tell you. It might give you ideas.'

'Oh, I have them already, believe me.' He sent her a look of such lust over the rim of his glass that she burst out laughing, even though her heart felt as if it were about to explode from her chest with sheer anticipation.

It took another hour before Kate managed to persuade the children up to bed, and still they whinged and moaned. But finally she did settle them down and returned to the sitting room, with a great deal of nervous trepidation, it had to be said, despite her resolve to allow herself the indulgence of an affair.

Ross had moved from the armchair in which he'd been sitting to the settee. Kate's heart raced, especially when he said, 'Come here,' holding one arm out to her. 'I've waited long enough. I only have so much patience, and it's running dangerously low at the moment.' His voice was throaty; throbbing with passion. 'Today was just the appetiser. Now I want the main course.'

Kate couldn't have spoken then if her very life had depended on it. She simply did as he'd asked and sat down by the side of him, her entire body feeling as if it were about to spontaneously combust. He didn't give her time to make any sort of protest — not that she wanted to. He gathered her close, wrapping both arms about her and bending her backwards until her head rested on the cushion in the corner, and he could bury his mouth into the hollow area of her neck, before bestowing feather-light kisses all over her arched throat.

'You smell of sun and sand, and — oh yes, the scent of suntan cream.' His amusement was only too evident.

'Oh, sorry!' Why hadn't she had a shower? she agonised. Supposing she smelled sweaty too? And her teeth, she should have brushed them ...

'Don't be. I like it. You smell gorgeous.' He moved his mouth upwards to tenderly kiss her ever-so-slightly sunburned cheek, her nose, and her eyelids, before finally lowering it again to her lips. The kiss that followed took every ounce of Kate's breath away. She'd believed the kisses at the beach had been as good as they got, but these went several stages further and were utterly mind-blowing, inducing such an avalanche of emotion within her that she feared for her sanity. She couldn't

192

stop her arms from sliding up his chest, so that her hands met at the back of his neck. His hair was thick and silky against her fingertips, his scalp smooth to the touch.

But then, out of the blue, he stopped and pulled back from her slightly. His gaze, as it rested upon her, darkened, and it was then that she saw the minute flecks appear. She recognised, in that second, what it was they indicated. Passion, pure and simple.

'Kate,' he softly said, 'are you sure about this? I don't want to pressure you.'

'Yes,' she softly said, 'I'm sure. Don't stop.'

'I won't, believe me, but do you think we could go to bed? This settee isn't really ... '

She didn't let him finish. She freed herself from his grasp, pulled her top back into place, and then, pushing him off her, stood up. His expression changed in an instant. He looked anxious, disturbed even, as he looked up at her. 'Sorry, have I ... Have I said the wrong thing?'

'No,' she murmured. 'You've echoed my thoughts exactly.' She held out a hand to him. 'Come on. Quietly, though. We don't want to wake the children.'

They tiptoed up the stairs like two naughty children trying to escape their parents' attention. When they reached the top, Kate quietly closed the children's bedroom doors, which she'd left ajar as she always did. After which, she led Ross into her own room with its comfortable king-sized bed.

For the first time, she felt unsure about what she was intending to do. She could feel Ross's gaze upon her face. It was a searching one, as if he'd detected her belated doubts.

'Kate?'

She swung and regarded him. His eyes were dark, velvety, gleaming. He moved quickly to her and encircled her with his arms.

'It's okay if you've changed your mind.'

'N-no, I haven't, not really. It's-it's just that I haven't done this in a while, and I only ever slept with Simon, in any case.

I'm not very experienced.'

'We'll take it slowly.' He guided her backwards to the foot of the bed, keeping his arms around her. Very gently, he lowered her down onto the duvet and then, bending her back to lie flat, he bent over her and began to kiss her again, with such heart-aching tenderness that her fear that she'd disappoint him vanished, and instead she felt the passion arise in her once more. And with that, everything was okay.

Ross began to make love to her, slowly, gently, gradually undressing her until she lay naked by the side of him. His expression as he looked at her told her how much he wanted her. 'You're so beautiful,' he murmured. With fingers that she could see were quivering, he removed his shirt and trousers, and then they lay, clinging to each other, their bodies perfectly attuned, fitting together as if this was what they'd been born to do.

When he finally took her completely, she felt the tears well in her eyes and begin to track their way down her face.

Tenderly, he kissed them away, whispering, 'It's all right, Kate. Everything's all right,' and he started to make love to her all over again.

Dawn had broken when they awoke, still wrapped in each other's arms; and it was then, as she heard the first birds begin to sing, and the rising sun sent its first rays through a small gap between the curtains, that the reality of it all hit Kate.

What had she done? How could she have been so thoughtless?

# 9

All Kate could think in that moment was that she'd allowed a man who had no idea of her real identity, who didn't know she was in the witness protection scheme, to make love to her, not just once but over and over, and then spend the remainder of the night with her.

She turned her head and looked at him. Her heart felt full, not only with love, but with a deep tenderness as well. She thought he was asleep, but as if sensing her gaze upon him, he opened his eyes and smiled at her.

'Good morning, my love.'

Grief almost overwhelmed her then. She couldn't do this. What had she been thinking? She couldn't go on lying to him, deceiving him, maybe putting him in danger too. It wasn't fair to him; it wasn't fair to Cleo. As he reached for her, she sat up, swinging her legs out of the bed, and grabbing her dressing gown from the nearby chair as she did so.

He too sat up. 'Hey, what's wrong?' He stood up then and quickly pulled his shirt and trousers on.

'I-I can't do this.' Kate also got to her feet and wrapped the dressing gown around her, pulling the belt tight. Naked, she felt too vulnerable; way too exposed. Every one of her emotions had risen to the surface and was fighting wildly for expression: desire, passion … love. She rigorously repressed them. She knew what she had to do and say. But did she have the strength, the determination to do it?

Somehow she started to speak. 'Please — will you go before the children?' Her voice broke and she felt the sting of tears. She turned her back on him, not wanting him to see her distress.

But Ross, being Ross, wasn't having any of that. He grasped her by her shoulders, turning her round to face him. His gaze seared into her. 'I'm not going anywhere till you tell me what's wrong.

I thought you wanted this as much as I did.'

But words were beyond Kate at that moment. What was she to do? She couldn't go on deceiving him, but she couldn't tell him the truth either. Oh God, what a bloody mess she'd created. Helplessly, she shook her head.

'Kate?' He tilted her face upwards with his index finger, so that she was looking straight at him.

'S-sorry. I can't.'

'You can't what?'

'I can't tell you.' She was very well aware that a few careless words revealing who she was could put an end to everything she'd built here, especially if the person she told subsequently spoke about it. And, as she belatedly admitted, she could also have put Ross and Cleo in danger with her incautious, impetuous behaviour. She'd spent the entire day with them, behaving as if they were a family, allowing them to get far too close. Dangerously so. If someone was indeed watching her, they'd have seen them all together. And what better weapon to use against her, to force her to remain silent about what she'd seen, than to threaten to hurt the very people she loved and cared about? Because she did care about them, both Cleo and Ross, just as much as she cared about Ellie and Matt.

Ross stared down at her then, his eyes narrowed. 'Are you regretting what we did? Is that it?'

It took her a few seconds to realise he'd just given her the perfect reason for ending things between them. 'Yes, I'm sorry but I do. We shouldn't have — I shouldn't have. It must have been the wine.'

He abruptly released her. His face had hardened; his mouth was a compressed line, his eyes chips of stone. 'Why shouldn't we? We're both responsible adults. And I don't believe you had so much wine that you didn't know what you were doing.' Belatedly, he looked doubtful. 'You are on the pill, aren't you?'

Oh jeez. No, she wasn't. Her heart beat with a sickening force. She'd stopped taking it after Simon died. There'd seemed no point in continuing.

'Well, obviously you aren't.' Ross's expression now was an even grimmer one. 'Well, that's as good a reason as any to regret what we did — several times.' He cocked his head and stared at her. 'So that's it then, is it? End of story for us?'

She nodded. 'Yes. I'm sorry, but I can't.'

'I know.' He bit out the words. 'You can't see me anymore. You can't do this again. But really, Kate, you should have thought of that before ...' He scornfully indicated the rumpled duvet. '... before allowing me into your bed. I didn't have you down as a tease.'

He despised her. The knowledge almost felled her. 'I'm not a tease,' she faintly protested, though she could quite see why he'd think that. And in that second, she wished she could simply curl up and die. No man had ever regarded her in such a manner.

'Oh, you're not? So how would you describe what you've just done?'

'T-there are reasons.'

'Really? I'd love to hear them, then. After all, you led me on all day yesterday.'

Stung by his accusation, Kate protested, 'No, I didn't.' They'd both wanted what had happened, him as well as her. He'd made that crystal clear, both with his words and his looks.

'Yes, you did.' His tone was a withering one. Kate felt something shrivel inside her. 'Melting looks, provocative smiles, letting me hold you on the beach, pressing yourself against me, kissing me. Oh, you led me on all right.' His jaw looked as if it had been chiselled from granite by this time. 'And then, back here, encouraging me to make love to you — and, bloody fool that I was, I fell for it. All of it.' He snorted, his scorn plain to see. Whether at himself or at her, she couldn't have said.

'It's not like that. I didn't deliberately lead you on.'

'Okay. So why the change of heart? I think I have a right to know, don't you?'

'I can't tell you.'

'For Christ's sake!' he shouted. 'You could pretty shortly be carrying my child.'

Her heart sank. He was right; absolutely right. 'Will you go now, please?' She was struggling to hold back the sobs that were so near to the surface; they were all but stopping the breath in her throat. 'You'll wake the children.'

'Right. If that's what you really want.' He remained quite still then, waiting for her to say something. To ask him to stay?

She couldn't do that. 'It is,' she softly told him. Her conscience wouldn't permit her to go on lying to him, so she did the only thing she could. She ended what had barely begun.

He continued to stare at her, his eyes so dark now they were almost black.

'Please ring me if you find out you're pregnant — at least do that for me.' And he swung away and strode from the bedroom.

It wasn't until she heard the front door close behind him that Kate sank down onto the bed and began to weep; a deep, heartbreaking anguish that finally engulfed and then crushed her.

She loved him so much, but she couldn't have him. Not until she could tell him the truth about herself. And that time was a long way off — if it ever came.

★   ★   ★

As if all that wasn't enough, Kate once again became aware of a briefly glimpsed presence whenever she was out of the house. As before, it was no more than a fleeting impression of a man turning a corner; but nevertheless, she had a constant sense of being followed, of someone always being there. Yet the moment she turned to look behind her, she could see no one.

Then one night, as she was preparing to go up to bed, she looked out of the sitting-room window and, finally, saw someone out there. It was a man standing motionless, staring across the road at her as he lifted a hand, pointed two fingers at her — just like the first time — and mimicked shooting her.

She grabbed the phone and rang Bob Turpin. With her words tumbling over each other, she told him what she'd just seen.

'I'll come round,' he said. 'Don't open the door to anyone. I'll ring the bell three times.'

Of course by the time he got there, which was actually only five minutes or so, maybe ten, the figure had vanished into the night, leaving empty shadows behind him.

'Are you sure he was watching you,' he asked, 'and not simply waiting for someone?'

'Why would he be doing that? There are no other houses here. But how the hell has he found me?'

'I don't know. In fact, it's so improbable as to be almost impossible.' He frowned at her. 'I'll get in touch with the powers that be. They'll probably suggest moving you.'

'No.' She was adamant. 'I'm not moving. We're settled here. The children are happy. I'm happy.'

But was she? She'd been miserable since the night she'd spent with Ross. He hadn't tried to contact her again, so she could only assume he'd given up on her. Brenda had told her that Dan, whom she was still seeing, had said that Ross was deeply troubled, and visibly unhappy. 'Did something happen between you two?'

'Not really,' Kate had told her, but she'd sensed Brenda hadn't believed her. 'I just thought it best to cool things down.'

Maybe it would be best to move on and begin again somewhere else. Ross clearly didn't want her, or surely, in spite of the way things had ended between them, he'd have got in touch. Moving away would help her forget him — wouldn't it?

'Cool things down?' Brenda was asking. 'How hot have they been, then?'

'I didn't mean it that way,' Kate protested. 'I'm simply not ready for a relationship.'

'And is that what Ross wanted?'

'I-I think so.'

'Jeez! And you've turned him down. Once again, I ask you, are you mad, woman?'

Kate ended the conversation by walking into the stockroom behind the shop, pretending she needed something. But she could feel Brenda's sceptical gaze following her.

To her relief, she hadn't seen the mysterious figure again, which led her to wonder if she'd imagined it all. It was beginning to feel highly likely. She was permanently on edge, her head ceaselessly throbbing with tension, the back of her neck stiff and painful. She was taking aspirin like it was going out of fashion in an effort to ease it, so, who knew, maybe she was hallucinating; visualising the thing she most feared? She smiled grimly. Maybe she was even beginning to lose her mind. In which case, Bob had been right to doubt her version of things. He hadn't got back to her about moving, anyway. She didn't know if she was pleased about that or not.

And then the thing she'd dreaded most looked as if it had indeed happened.

Her period was overdue, and as she was always pretty regular, she knew she was probably pregnant. She stopped taking the aspirin immediately — not that it had eased her pain, in any case. But it wasn't just that which was troubling her. Ellie and Matt were constantly asking when they were going to see Ross and Cleo again, and moaned and grumbled when she replied she didn't know.

'Can't you ring him?' Ellie demanded at one point.

'No, I can't,' Kate sharply responded. Between her and Brenda, who was also nagging her about seeing Ross and putting the poor man out of his misery, she felt as if she had no free will of her own anymore.

Ellie had eyed her, her head to one side. 'Have you two had a row?'

She sounded far too grown up for a ten-year-old. What was she — and Matt — going to think about their mother having Ross's baby? Kate had a sneaking suspicion that Ellie at least would be thrilled, if not ecstatic. She'd always wanted another baby in the family; an addition she'd be old enough now to mother, to push around in a buggy. But Matt? He'd been the baby of the family for eight years and would be unlikely to want to relinquish that advantage. And, oh God, what about Cleo? Kate closed her eyes in despair. She couldn't imagine the girl would be pleased. She'd most likely revert to her initially scornful view of Kate — and Ellie, probably, if she made her happiness at the unexpected news too apparent.

But for now, all she said was, 'No. A little disagreement, that's all.'

On the whole, though, life carried on as normal, apart from a feeling of nausea in the mornings. And then Kate and Morwenna met for one of their occasional midweek evenings out. Morwenna took one look at her and asked, 'What's wrong? You look terrible. Are you coming down with something?'

'No, I just feel a bit under the weather, that's all.'

'Are you sure?'

'Yes.' But she was far from sure; in fact, she was horribly afraid, and had no idea how she was going to cope. The truth was, she couldn't deny any longer that she was pregnant. Her breasts were sore and enlarged, and she'd been sick the past few mornings — all symptoms that she remembered from her other two pregnancies.

'Okay. I'll get the drinks in, then. Your usual red wine?'

'No,' Kate hastily said. 'Just a tonic water, please.'

Morwenna looked at her, her concern clear to see. 'Kate, you can tell me. Something's wrong, I can see. You're deathly pale and you've got dark rings under your eyes.'

'I think I'm pregnant,' Kate blurted.

For the first time since she'd known Morwenna, her friend was lost for words. Finally she said, 'Well, you sure know how to drop a bombshell.'

'Sorry.' Kate managed an apologetic grin.

'How have you got yourself pregnant?

210

Presuming you are, of course.'

'Well, that's the thing. I didn't get myself pregnant. Someone else did that for me.'

'Okay, smart alec. So who … Oh my God.' Morwenna lifted a hand to her mouth. 'Ross.' Kate nodded. 'But why? I mean — when did you do the deed?'

'Five weeks ago.'

'I didn't even know you were seeing him.'

'I wasn't … not really. It was just the one time.' It hadn't been, of course. It had been three or four times, without contraception, all in the same night. She couldn't have been more negligent if she deliberately tried. But she wasn't about to tell Morwenna that.

'Bloody hell. That was a bit of bad luck. Where did this happen?'

'We'd been out for the day with the kids, and-and he came back to the cottage. And well, it just sort of happened.'

'No protection then, obviously.'

Kate shook her head. 'He assumed I was on the pill.'

'And you aren't?'

'No. I hadn't anticipated having an affair. I didn't even think about protection.'

'Well, it was hardly an affair if it was just once.'

'Oh Morwenna, what should I do? I can't abort it, I just can't.'

'Does Ross know?'

'No, but I'll have to tell him. It won't be long before it becomes noticeable, anyway.'

Morwenna looked over Kate's shoulder towards the entrance of the pub. 'Well here's your chance. Ross has just walked in — with a woman, no less.' She looked shocked, more shocked than Kate had ever seen her. 'What a bastard. He gets one woman pregnant and then goes out with another. He hasn't wasted any time,' she scoffed. 'Morals of a tom cat, obviously. I'd thought better of him.'

Kate closed her eyes in sheer mortification. Wasn't this just her luck — that Ross should walk in. If her friend had noticed her pallor, then for sure he would. There wasn't much he missed. In which case, would he guess? He'd be bound to. He was far from stupid; he'd proved that time and time again.

Just as she'd expected he would, the second he spotted her and Morwenna he strode over, clearly abandoning his female companion at the bar. 'Morwenna,' he said with a curt nod. 'Kate?'

Reluctantly, Kate looked up at him. His expression instantly sharpened as his eyes narrowed at her. He scrutinised her keenly, taking in her pallor and heavy-eyed expression. 'You don't look well. What's wrong?'

'I'm fine.' She looked away, not wanting to see the dawning awareness of her condition.

'Okay. If you say so. I'll ring you tomorrow.'

She did look at him then; she couldn't stop herself. And, just as she'd feared, saw the steeliness in his eye; the certainty that she was carrying his child. Still, she tried to protest: 'That's really not necessary.'

'I think it is.' His jaw hardened in the way she'd grown so familiar with as he glanced down at her glass of tonic water, then looked back directly into her eyes. 'Have a good evening.' He strode back to rejoin his female companion.

An agonising stab of sheer jealousy pierced Kate in that moment, as images of the two of them in bed floated before her eyes. Would he make love to her as tenderly as he had to Kate?

'He knows,' Morwenna murmured.

'Yes.'

# 10

The rest of the evening passed in a blur for Kate as she struggled against the almost irresistible need to keep glancing at Ross and his attractive companion; a need that intensified each time she sensed his gaze upon her. In the end, she was heartily glad when the two of them departed. Not long after that, she suggested that she and Morwenna also leave, and was equally glad when her friend readily agreed.

Morwenna drove Kate back to the cottage and picked up Pattie, who'd been babysitting. The schools had broken up for the summer and she needed to earn some money, she'd told Kate, before going back to begin the A-level studies she'd need to obtain a place at university. She came to the cottage on the three days Kate worked, and took care of Ellie and Matt.

But despite Kate feeling totally exhausted — again, she remembered the feeling throughout her other two pregnancies — that night she had very little sleep, and she was up at six thirty the next morning being very sick. There could be no question that she was carrying Ross's baby. She didn't imagine he'd be any happier than she was about that, not after the manner in which they'd parted that last time.

The children hadn't woken yet. She was sitting on the settee, drinking a cup of green tea and trying to suppress the nausea that was yet again surging, when the doorbell rang. She checked the clock. It was just after seven fifteen. She wasn't even dressed; hadn't had the energy, in fact. Who could it be at this time of the morning?

She walked to the front door and gingerly opened it just an inch. She saw Ross standing there — the very last person she'd expected to see on her doorstep so early in the morning. His expression was a dark one, his brow pulled down into a frown.

'When were you planning to tell me?' he angrily demanded.

'T-tell you wh-what?'

'What the hell do you think? That you're pregnant.' He stepped inside, not quite pushing her out of the way, but moving her firmly to one side. He slammed the door behind himself, and Kate turned to walk back into the sitting room. Before she could do so, however, a massive surge of sickness washed over her, making her lurch around and make a run for the stairs. She leapt up them, two at a time, and ran into the bathroom. She only just made it and was already kneeling over the toilet bowl, retching miserably and desperately trying to stem the flood of tears that came with it, when Ross strode in behind her.

'Oh God. Kate, Kate.' He knelt by her side, holding her hair away from her face and mouth, and gently rubbing her back until she'd finished throwing up. Then he half-turned her, pulled her into his arms, and gently said, 'I'm sorry.'

With that, Kate surrendered to her abject misery and, gratefully leaning into him, began to quietly weep. He gathered her close, putting both arms around her, cradling her as she sobbed. The knowledge that she was probably stinking of vomit into the bargain didn't help her state of mind one bit. But if Ross noticed, he gave no indication of it.

'Sweetheart,' he soothed as he began to gently rock her. 'It's all right. I'm here. Everything's going to be all right.'

But Kate knew it wasn't. She pulled away from him. 'I'm okay — really.'

He bent his head so that he could look directly at her. 'You are pregnant, I take it? You might as well tell me. I'll see for myself sooner or later.'

'Yes. And-and ... ' She began to weep again. 'It's my own fault. If I'd been on the pill ... '

'But the fact is,' he gently told her, 'you weren't, and I should've checked first. I was totally irresponsible. It wasn't just your fault. But I was so blinded with wanting you, nothing else mattered.'

She hiccupped as her sobs began to subside. He tugged her back into his arms. 'Ssh, ssh. We'll cope with it, the two of us — together.'

She stared up at him, her eyes wide and translucent with the remnants of her tears. 'What do you mean?'

'I mean it's my baby as much as yours, and I'm here for you. I want to be involved.' He paused, eyeing her, his lack of certainty plain to see. 'I-I want us to get married. I love you, Kate, and I think — no, I'm pretty sure — you love me. Hmmm?'

She freed herself, knowing it was hard for her to think, let alone speak rationally, while his arms were around her. She stared at him, aghast that he could even suggest such a thing. 'M-marry you?' she finally stammered. 'B-but what about the woman you were with last evening?'

'A business associate, that's all.'

'Oh.' Kate was speechless. She'd spent the better part of the night imagining all sorts of things, mostly picturing them in bed together. And all the woman had been was a business associate. She'd put herself through all that pain and anguish for nothing.

'Please, Kate, at least think about it. You must have realised how I feel about you?'

But Kate's head was spinning, her thoughts racketing around. How could she agree to marry him? He was right — she did love him. She was crazy about him. But still, he didn't even know her real name; didn't know she'd been threatened by a hardened criminal, a murderer. Even if she told him the truth, how could she marry him and drag him into her mess? Possibly place him in danger, too?

'No, I can't.'

'Why not? We're both free.'

'I can't. It's impossible. But I won't shut you out.'

He got to his feet then. 'You won't shut me out? What the blazes does that mean? It's my child too.'

Kate, too, now struggled to her feet. 'Keep your voice down. The children are still asleep.'

But she was too late. Matt called, 'Mummy, where are you?' And before she could answer, the little boy ran into the bathroom, still rubbing sleep from his eyes. Naturally, Ellie swiftly followed suit. 'Ross!' she cried. 'Why are you here?'

'I came to see your mummy. Nothing to worry about.'

But Ellie continued to study them both, suspicion gleaming in her eyes. 'Did you stay the night?'

'No. I've just arrived.'

'Why?'

'I needed to talk to your mummy.'

'In the bathroom?'

Kate and Ross both ignored that question, mainly because neither had an answer. At least, not one that Ellie would believe.

'Are you going to have breakfast with us?' Matt asked.

'No, 'fraid not. I have a meeting so I have to go.' He looked at Kate then, his eyes steely with determination. 'I'll come back this evening. We need to talk about

221

this. Eight o'clock, okay?'

Kate could see there was absolutely no point in arguing with him. He was like a bulldozer; there was no refusing him. 'Okay,' she said.

'Right. Bye, you two. You'll probably be in bed when I arrive, so I'll see you some other time. Maybe next weekend.'

Kate was tempted to say 'No way', but didn't have the heart — or the energy. So she remained silent.

'Goody,' both children said. 'Goody, goody.'

★　★　★

Somehow Kate managed to crawl into work that morning. Brenda took one look at her and said, 'Oh, dear me. If that's some sort of bug you've got, you'd better go back home again. I can't afford to be ill.'

'No, it isn't. I'll be fine.'

But she wasn't, and by one o'clock she was forced to say to Brenda, 'I think I will have to go, Bren. Do you mind?'

'No. You're about as much use here as a sugar mouse in a rainstorm.'

Kate stumbled to her car. Fortunately she'd managed to find a parking space near the shop, so she didn't have to go far. She then drove home. The children and Pattie were out somewhere, so thankfully she went to bed and slept for two hours. By the time she awoke again, they were back, so she got up and told Pattie she could go home.

'Are you sure?' Pattie asked her. 'You don't look too good.'

'I'm fine. I've not been sleeping well, so I'm exhausted.'

In an effort to drive what were beginning to feel like completely unresolvable worries from her mind, she switched on the television news channel. Halfway through, one particular report had her almost catatonic with shock.

'Robert Wilmot, the man accused of stabbing Andy Hayes, a leading member of a notorious Birmingham gang, was this morning found dead in his cell. It seems that he had a plastic bag over his head

223

and was asphyxiated. There is a question over whether it was suicide or murder. The other members of Andy Hayes's gang had apparently sworn vengeance on Robert Wilmot, himself a gangland criminal, and had bragged about having contacts in the same prison. That statement has yet to be verified.'

Kate slumped back onto the settee. This meant she wouldn't have to give evidence, didn't it? It could also mean that she and the children could come out of the witness protection scheme. Hope sprang up within her. It could still all be all right. Everything was going to be okay.

She rang Bob and asked if he'd seen the news. He had, but he'd already been informed in any case.

'Does this mean I can leave the witness protection scheme?'

'I don't know. You could still be in danger from his gangland contacts. They're usually keen to take revenge.'

'But his death's nothing to do with me.'

'I know, but be patient. I'll be in touch.'

Kate's disappointment at his lukewarm

response was acute. She busied herself preparing the children's supper and getting them bathed prior to going to bed. They were both sleepy, so they didn't protest when she took them upstairs, and within minutes they were both asleep.

She returned to the kitchen and made herself a cup of tea. Between the shock of the news she'd heard and her own sickness, she didn't feel hungry. She still needed to eat, however, so she made do with a bowl of soup. She'd just finished it when the doorbell rang. She glanced at the clock. Ross was early. It was only a quarter to eight. She walked to the door and opened it.

It wasn't Ross standing there. It was a stranger. A tall man — at least six feet, heavily built, and with a pockmarked face. He had tattoos on every inch of exposed skin, and rings through his ears. A heavy gold chain hung round his muscular neck.

'Yes?' Her voice quivered as her heart raced.

'Kate Summers?' he demanded.

She stared at him. His eyes were dilated and he twitched continually. He was visibly under the influence of some sort of drug.

Without answering, she tried to close the door on him. But he reached out and held it open. 'Don't you shut the door on me,' he yelled. He forced it even wider and pushed himself inside, knocking her out of his way before he slammed it closed with one foot. He then made a grab for her arm and pushed her in front of him into the sitting room.

'Hey,' she cried, 'who are you? What do you want?' She tugged herself free of his grip.

A rising nausea that had nothing at all to do with her pregnancy was telling her that something was seriously wrong, just as a terrible suspicion began to take hold of her. Thank God the children were in bed and out of harm's way. At least, she desperately hoped so.

'What do you want?' she again asked.

'Have you heard the news?' he growled.

'Yes.' Fear engulfed her then. He could

only be referring to Robert Wilmot's death.

'So you've heard that Rob's been murdered?'

'If you mean Robert somebody-or-other, then yes — on the six o'clock news. He-he was found dead in his prison cell this morning. B-but what's that got to do with me?' She was barely able to get the words out. This man knew who she was and what her connection was to Robert Wilmot, which meant he was most probably the one who'd been stalking her, trying to scare and intimidate her. His presence here couldn't mean anything else.

His next words confirmed that. He leant towards her, thrusting his face almost into hers. His breath was rank. 'You stupid cow.' Droplets of saliva splashed the skin of her face. She flinched back from him. 'It's all your fault. I know who you really are. You're Annie Harvey. If you hadn't gone to the police —' He stabbed a finger at her. '— Rob wouldn't have been arrested, he wouldn't have been locked up, and he'd still be alive now.'

She took a couple of steps back from him. 'I-I don't know wh-what you're talking about. I'm Kate Summers.'

'Don't give me that load of fucking bullshit. I've come to hand out justice.' He pulled a plastic bag from his pocket and waved it in front of her. 'It's either this or this.' He then pulled a knife from his other pocket and held it up before her. It wasn't large, but the slender blade looked extremely sharp.

Again, she flinched away from him. He gave a triumphant, gloating smile. 'Yeah, I can see you understand me. He died, so you're going to die the same way he did. Your children will find you in the morning. That's your punishment.'

Kate viewed both items in horror. 'No — please,' she whispered. 'His death is nothing to do with me.' Her body was stiff with terror now. She glanced wildly around for her mobile phone, only to see it on the opposite side of the room, on the mantelpiece and well out of reach. Her heart lurched and then sank. She had to get to it somehow and ring the number Bob had given her. It was her only hope. Should she make a dash for it? Or would he stab her on the way? And even if she got to the phone, how would she make the call without his seeing what she was doing and stopping her?

But she knew she had to try. It was her only chance of coming out of this alive. She started forward, but it was hopeless. He simply reached out and grabbed hold of her. He then pushed her down onto the settee. She sprawled backwards into the corner, too terrified to move again. All she could think was that her children were upstairs in bed. Supposing they heard what was going on and came down?

Laying the knife down on the arm of the settee, the man opened the bag, preparing to put it over her head.

'No, wait — please — don't do this. You don't need to, not now. There won't be a trial.'

But he ignored her and forced the bag over her head, clamping it round her throat with his hands. She tried to scream, but couldn't. The plastic clung to her face and mouth, cutting off her breath and stopping her from making any sound at all. Frantically, she tore at it with her fingernails, trying to pull it off, to tear a hole, anything to get some air. But it was impossible. Her breathing grew more laboured. She was going to die. Possibly within minutes.

The doorbell rang. 'Who's that?' the man demanded.

Kate tried to speak, and failed. The plastic still clung to her face. She was having even greater difficulty breathing. Her vision was clouding … Mercifully then, he pulled the bag off, only to grab the knife again. She gasped hungrily at the air, breathing as deeply and quickly as she could, re-inflating her lungs. 'I-I don't know.'

'Go to the door and get rid of whoever it is. If you don't — remember your kids upstairs. You don't want anything to happen to them.' He picked up the knife and waved it in front of her. 'I'll be listening to every word.'

Oh God — now he was threatening the children. She glanced wildly around, desperately seeking inspiration. She had to stop him. The person at the door must be Ross. Again her thoughts raced. How could she alert him to what was happening without endangering them all, especially the children? A signal of some sort? But what? Her wretched brain was refusing to perform. All she knew was that she couldn't put her children in harm's way. She'd rather die herself along with her unborn child. She had to do as he said.

Slowly she walked into the hall and opened the door. Sure enough, it was Ross.

'Kate?' His expression sharpened as he stared at her, taking in her pallor, her heaving chest, her tortured breathing. 'What's wrong?'

She widened her eyes at him, mutely trying to convey to him all what was happening.

'Are you feeling sick? You're as white as a sheet.' He moved towards her, his arms reaching out for her.

She jerked backwards. He frowned at her. 'No — sorry, I can't talk now.' Then it came to her. 'Will you tell Brenda I can't make it?' *Please, God, let him decode what I'm telling him as a plea for help.* He'd surely realise there was something wrong. She wouldn't normally be asking him to give a message to Brenda.

'What?' He frowned again, his expression a mixture of confusion and anxiety. 'Brenda?'

She swivelled her eyes sideways, at the same time jerking her head fractionally backwards, as she desperately sought to convey the fact that someone else was inside. She put a finger to her mouth, warning him to speak softly.

'Something's wrong?' Ross slowly mouthed the words as his eyes narrowed at her.

She nodded, praying the intruder wasn't watching her. She could almost see Ross's mind working as he tried to comprehend what was happening; what she was trying to tell him. He muttered beneath his breath, 'Someone else is here?'

She whispered, 'Yes, and he's got a knife.'

'Christ,' he swore softly. 'Tell me quickly. What's happening?'

She shook her head to indicate she couldn't say any more.

The intruder called, 'Kate — darling, what are you doing?'

Ross leant close to her, as if he were about to kiss her goodbye, and muttered, 'Is the back door unlocked? And the side gate open?'

Thankful that she hadn't yet locked up, she muttered back, 'Yes.'

The man inside called again, 'Are you coming?'

'Yes,' she called back. She indicated with her hand that she'd go back into the sitting room and promptly closed the front door. She then returned to the stranger.

'That took long enough. What did he want?'

'He brought a message from a friend

of mine.'

'He's gone now?' The man went to the window and looked out.

Kate held her breath. If Ross didn't return to his car ... But she heard the sound of the engine firing up and the noise of a heavy vehicle moving off.

'Good,' the stranger said. 'He's gone.' He looked back at Kate again.

She gave a tiny sigh. Ross had taken the precaution of moving the car before hopefully parking it somewhere out of sight and returning to gain access to the cottage. She hoped and prayed it wouldn't take long, otherwise he'd be too late to save her.

The intruder pushed her back down onto the settee. He was holding the knife and the bag in the same hand now. She noticed that her mobile phone had disappeared. He must have taken it while she was at the front door, in order to make sure she couldn't call anyone. He gave her a grin, which actually wasn't a grin at all, but more of a grimace, and said, 'Better start praying, because you ain't gonna be

here much longer. You're gonna to die
— I promise you that.'

# 11

'Wait!' Kate cried. Somehow she had to stall him. Get him talking. Give Ross the time he needed to return with some sort of plan. And — please, God — he would. It shouldn't take too long if he decided to ring the police before coming back — but she could be dead by then. Frantic to delay things, she quickly started talking. 'Tell me — I'm curious. How did you know where I was? Nobody knew, not even my family.'

He took the bait. 'Yeah, well, it was clever really.' She watched as his chest swelled with pride. 'A good mate of mine is very friendly with a cop back in Birmingham. He's worked with us before, helping us out for a suitable sum of money.' He winked at her as if they were close buddies. 'He wouldn't let on at first where you were, and all we knew was that you'd upped and disappeared. Actually, I don't think he knew at that point. But a few quickly arranged crooked games of poker soon had him owing thousands to a couple of extremely nasty individuals, and that made him very keen to get us the info we needed in order to pay his debt. I don't know how he did it, but he did. Someone talked who shouldn't have. But then, there's always somebody ready to tell you what you need to know, even in the police force, for the right money.

'It didn't take that long, actually, and hey presto, I was here. I watched the cottage until I got a good look at you and was sure I'd recognise you outside the house. Then I followed you round town, making sure you caught enough glimpses of me to let you know you'd been found, and so scare you into not giving evidence in court. It would've worked, too, because I could tell you were getting spooked. Did you enjoy the car chase? And what about the wreath, eh? I bet that really scared you.' He leered at her, his gaze lingering lustfully upon her breasts. 'Pity I've got to do away with you, because you're a good-looking bird. We could have some fun.'

Kate shuddered at the notion. Fun, with this repulsive individual? She'd rather poke her eyes out with pins than allow him to lay a single finger on her.

'But now that Rob's been murdered, and his family and mates want justice for him,' he went on, 'well, you see the position I'm in. It needs to be a life for a life.' He shrugged, as if the whole thing was immaterial to him.

'I see.' Kate tried to ignore the sensation of terror that was filling her at his careless attitude to murder by listening intently for any sound from the kitchen. If Ross didn't come back …

But then she heard the faint click of the back door opening. He was in. If she could just keep this man talking, just a little while longer, it would give Ross the time to work out what to do. At least she'd managed to warn him that the man had a knife, so he'd be prepared.

She was facing the door into the hallway and it was open, so she could see

Ross as he stood motionless, listening intently to what was going on. He was holding the carving knife in one hand, obviously intending to use it as a weapon if necessary.

'Anyway,' her assailant went on, 'enough of all that. It's time for justice to be served.' He laid the knife down on the arm of the settee that was furthest from Kate's reach.

Ross was still standing, taking in the scene. His gaze went to the plastic bag which the man was holding, so he saw the exact second that it was slipped over Kate's head. He moved so quickly then that the stranger had no time to react. He grabbed hold of him and pressed the blade of the knife against his throat. 'Let her go,' he commanded, 'and then lie on the floor, face down.' Taken completely by surprise, the man didn't put up any sort of fight, and did what Ross told him.

Ross then knelt by his side. 'Arms above your head and hands flat on the floor,' he again ordered. When the man did this, he placed a knee onto the middle of his back, while holding the blade of the knife against the nape of his neck. With his free hand, he held the intruder's left shoulder down on the floor. 'Ring for help, Kate — now.'

She tore the bag from her head and gasped, 'He's got my phone. It's got the number I need to ring on speed dial.'

She saw the questioning look that Ross gave her, but he didn't hesitate. He quickly thrust a hand into one of the man's trouser pockets and, as luck would have it, it was the right one. He pulled out Kate's phone. She grabbed it and stabbed the button for the number that Bob had given her. She heard it ring out twice. She ended the call, and then did exactly the same thing again, praying that Bob would hear it and respond. She then joined Ross in restraining the man on the floor. She did this by sitting on his legs. Between the two of them, he couldn't move.

To her relief, Bob had heard her call, because suddenly there was the sound of cars pulling up outside. She ran to the window and saw several armed response officers climbing out of three unmarked cars. Kate ran to open the door and they poured inside. 'Armed police, armed police!' they shouted, just as she'd seen on the television umpteen times. It all felt surreal, as if it were a drama being enacted in front of her.

'He's in there,' she said, pointing towards the sitting-room door. She followed them as they shouted, 'Stay down!'

Kate was on the verge of weeping, so great was her relief. She ran into the room just in time to see Ross getting to his feet and two of the officers haul the intruder to his feet and handcuff him, at the same time reading him his rights. The others were standing in a circle around them, weapons at the ready, all aimed at the stranger.

He turned his head and glared venomously at Kate, still standing in the doorway before snarling, 'Don't think this is the end of it, because it isn't. If it's not me ... ' He glanced sideways at the men holding him still. ' ... it'll be somebody else who'll come for you. It's just a matter of time. You'll never feel safe, ever again.'

★   ★   ★

Once the officers had left, taking the man who'd given his name as Nick Dawes with them, Ross turned to her, his face white, his eyes dark with shock. 'I think you owe me some sort of explanation,' he said, 'because it's clear you aren't who you say you are. Are you working undercover for the police? They arrived pretty bloody quickly.'

'No.'

'Mummy, Mummy!' It was Matt, calling from the upstairs landing.

'Yes, darling, I'm here,' she called back.

'What's that noise? Who's there?'

She glanced at Ross and said, 'Excuse me. I'll have to go up to him.'

'Of course. I'll wait here.'

Kate ran up the stairs, taking them two at a time, to find Ellie also out of her room and holding on to Matt's hand. 'Who were all those men?' she demanded. 'I looked out of my window.'

'It's okay, really. They were men who came to help me. There's nothing to worry about. Ross is here.'

'Ross, Ross!' Ellie called.

He appeared at the foot of the stairs. 'I'm here. You're okay.'

'Come up here, please.' Ellie was sounding tearful now, and she held her arms out to him. As if following her lead, Matt too began to cry.

'Hey, hey.' Ross swiftly ran up to them all. The children threw themselves at him. He lifted Matt up into his arms and then put an arm around Ellie's shoulders as she clung to him, her arms around his hips. 'Ssh, ssh,' he soothed, holding her close. 'I'm not going anywhere. Promise.'

Eventually, between them, Ross and Kate managed to coax the children back into their beds. Then, once they were settled, Ross took hold of Kate's hand and led her back downstairs. They went into the sitting room. Kate sat in one of the armchairs, while Ross took the settee.

He simply looked at her for a couple of moments, his expression grim and full of accusation, before he said, 'Okay. So if you aren't an undercover police officer, what are you?' His gaze was a hooded one now. Even so, she detected his suspicion of her. 'MI5?'

'It's nothing like that. I-I'm in witness protection.'

'What?' His eyes widened, every trace of accusation gone. It had been replaced by sheer astonishment; disbelief, even. 'Why?'

'I witnessed a murder — back in Birmingham. A man was stabbed, and I saw it happen. The murderer, a gangster called Robert Wilmot, saw me watching, and when I ran he followed me home. H-he stood outside my house and mimed shooting me. Which I took for a threat — that if I told anyone what I'd seen, he'd kill me.'

'Jesus.'

'He was found dead in his cell this morning with a polythene bag over his head. You might have heard it on the news.' Ross nodded. 'Nick Dawes, the man who was here, said he wanted justice. Or a life for a life, as he put it. Robert Wilmot was his mate, and I was the one responsible for his arrest, and so his subsequent death as well. Apparently.' She swallowed.

'My God, Kate. If I hadn't arrived when I did ... '

'He'd have killed me.' Speaking her worst fear out loud made her put both hands over her face. Realising how very close she'd been to death, she began to quietly weep, the tears flowing fast enough to seep between her clasped fingers. 'And my children too, in all likelihood,' she managed to sob. 'H-he's been stalking me, never quite in plain sight. I'd just get a feeling of someone being there, a glimpse from the corner of my eye. He made several silent phone calls; sent an anonymous letter threatening me if I spoke out about what I'd witnessed. He chased me in a car one evening. I had the children in the back. He sent a funeral wreath. It's been awful,' she sobbed. 'And then tonight he turned up and I-I thought it was you, so I opened the door.'

'Why the hell didn't you tell me any of this before?'

'I couldn't. I couldn't tell anyone, not even my family. They have no idea where I am. That's the condition the police make for your protection.'

'Well, it explains your reluctance to talk about your family,' he quietly said. 'I sensed there was something wrong, but I imagined it was a row. I never for a second considered anything like this.' He regarded her, his brow lowered in a frown. 'But haven't you had anyone from the protection scheme looking out for you? Did you tell them what was happening?'

'Yes. Well, some of it, not all.' She grimaced ruefully. 'My liaison officer is someone called Bob Turpin. But I didn't want to have to move again, which I suspected they'd have insisted on if they'd realised the extent of what was happening, so I didn't tell them. And I did wonder if it was all in my own head — that because I felt so vulnerable, I was seeing things.' She stopped talking. She'd been so stupid, placing them all in danger by not telling Bob what was happening to her.

'You didn't tell them? At least, not all of it?'

'No. But I did have an emergency number to ring. I had to ring it twice, end the call, and then do the same thing again. That way he'd know I was in trouble and needed help urgently. And, well, you saw the rest.'

'I'm beginning to understand now why you wouldn't let me get too close.' He managed a shaky smile.

She nodded. 'I couldn't. And then, that evening I met you at Morwenna's ... well, at first I thought you were Robert Wilmot. You look so much like him. I was scared stiff, until logic kicked in and I knew you couldn't be him. He was in prison.'

Ross looked genuinely shocked. 'You thought I was a murderer? No wonder you wouldn't agree to come out with me.' His eyes were almost black as he looked at her and muttered, 'Well, I don't think I've ever been mistaken for a murderer before.'

'As I said, I quickly realised how stupid I was being. But I did ring Bob to check that he hadn't escaped. He hadn't.'

'Well, that's a relief,' Ross drily remarked.

'I'm sorry. I wanted to tell you, so much, but I couldn't. And when I couldn't be honest with you, I decided I'd have to end things. I couldn't in all conscience go on deceiving you, and I couldn't be sure that I wouldn't be placing you and Cleo in danger. He or his gang could have used you in some way to make me refuse to give evidence.'

Ross tilted his head to one side and asked, 'So where does this leave us now?'

She regarded him in silence for a moment and then softly said, 'Wherever you want it to.'

'In that case ...' Something glinted in his eye, something that caused Kate's heart to wildly lurch. '... come here. I so badly want to make love to you. You've put me through seven shades of hell these past weeks.'

She smiled at him. 'I know the feeling.'

'So come here.' His voice throbbed with passion.

Kate didn't argue; she simply went. He pulled her into his arms and held her close. 'I love you, Kate.' He stopped talking abruptly. 'What *is* your real name?'

'Annabel. Annie for short.'

'I think I prefer Kate.'

'Then Kate I'll be. I've got used to it anyway. I probably wouldn't revert to Annie.'

His mouth stopped any further words as he kissed her with so much love, so much passion, yet with such tenderness she couldn't doubt his feelings for her.

Much later, he lifted his head and said, 'Now seems like a good time to repeat my proposal. Marry me. You clearly need someone to take care of you, and love aside, it will change your name again — legitimately, this time — making it doubly difficult for anyone to find you. In fact, if you want, we could move somewhere else. Abroad, even.'

'I'm sure that won't be necessary,' Kate

demurred. 'I'll ring Bob tomorrow and see what he thinks. But I really don't want to move, and I'm sure the children won't — well, other than to Bodruggan House, of course, with you. We've all made friends here; good friends.' She glanced flirtatiously up at him. 'And my answer to your proposal, by the way, is — yes, I will marry you.'

His heavy-lidded gaze moved over her face. 'In that case, do you think we could creep up the stairs to your comfortable bed, and I can love you properly?'

'Yes, yes, please. I love you — so very much.'

His eyes darkened with emotion. 'Good. We'll tell the children in the morning — and also tell them they'll be having a new little brother or sister.' He eyed her then, with more than a little uncertainty. 'Do you think they'll mind? It's a bit much to take it all in at once.'

'They'll be thrilled,' Kate said. 'They've well and truly taken you into their hearts, and Ellie has long wanted a baby in the family. And if it's a boy, Matt will be over the moon.' She frowned. 'But equally as important — how will Cleo take it?'

'Cleo will be pleased. She took to all of you as well. Like Ellie, she's always wanted brothers and sisters, so now she'll have them. Three of them. In fact, we'll wait and tell them all together, shall we?'

'Of course — and I'll ring my mother with the news. I guarantee that after she's recovered from the shock of it all, she and my sister will be here within a day or two.'

Ross regarded her with a frown. 'Do you think you maybe ought to hold back from telling people, even your family, where you are? And *who* you are, in the case of friends? Wait for your liaison officer to give you the go-ahead? You don't want to put yourself or the children in any further danger. And Dawes did say someone else would be after you.'

'I doubt that. I'm sure he just wanted to scare me. But, well, maybe I'll just tell my family. They won't pass it on to anyone else. And as you said, my married name will be different anyway, as will my address. And if I don't tell my liaison officer where I am either, or my new name, no one can talk this time.'

'Ah, I wondered how he'd managed to find you.'

'I'll tell you all about that some other time. Right now, I've got other more pressing needs.'

'Okay.' Ross all of a sudden sounded extremely pleased. 'So it all means the wedding must take place as quickly as possible.'

'I agree. Let's keep it very quiet and just do it. In a registry office. Just us and the children. Both of our families, of course, and maybe Morwenna and Brenda, but they'll be the only friends. Oh, and Brett and the girls. We can't leave them out.'

Ross gave a shout of laughter. 'If I've counted up correctly, that's already fourteen or so guests.'

Kate gave a rueful smile.

'It's okay; that's still a very small wedding. The important thing is we marry — quickly. I'll make enquiries first thing tomorrow and see what can be arranged.

Maybe there will have been a cancellation, and we can take that date, if we're lucky. But apart from that, I think you and the children should move in with me and Cleo, anyway. That way I can be sure you're all safe.'

With that settled, they quietly climbed the stairs to bed, where they made love until dawn was beginning to break and Ross finally slept. Kate lay awake — she was far too happy to sleep — listening to the first bird of the day begin to sing. It seemed to herald not just a new dawn, but also a new future, and she felt absolutely confident that from this moment on all would be well in her and her children's world.

But for the moment, she groaned softly; she needed to get to the bathroom immediately. She was starting to feel sick. She quietly and quickly climbed from bed and headed for the loo. But she wasn't quiet enough, because within seconds of her leaning over the toilet basin, Ross was at her side, his arm around her waist, supporting her, holding her. And somehow, despite her rising nausea, she managed to turn her head and smile at him, thinking to herself, *This is real love.* There was nothing more she could ask for. She had all she'd ever want.

We do hope that you have enjoyed reading this large print book.

Did you know that all of our titles are available for purchase?

We publish a wide range of high quality large print books including:
**Romances, Mysteries, Classics**
**General Fiction**
**Non Fiction and Westerns**

Special interest titles available in large print are:
**The Little Oxford Dictionary**
**Music Book, Song Book**
**Hymn Book, Service Book**

Also available from us courtesy of Oxford University Press:
**Young Readers' Dictionary**
**(large print edition)**
**Young Readers' Thesaurus**
**(large print edition)**

For further information or a free brochure, please contact us at:
**Ulverscroft Large Print Books Ltd.,**
**The Green, Bradgate Road, Anstey,**
**Leicester, LE7 7FU, England.**
**Tel:** (00 44) **0116 236 4325**
**Fax:** (00 44) **0116 234 0205**

# MIDSUMMER MAGIC

## Julie Coffin

Fearing that her ex-husband plans to take their daughter away with him to New Zealand, Lauren escapes with little Amy to the remote Cornish cottage bequeathed to her by her Great-aunt Hilda. But Lauren had not even been aware of Hilda's existence until now, so why was the house left to her and not local schoolteacher Adam Poldean, who seemed to be Hilda's only friend? Lauren sets out to learn the answers — and finds herself becoming attracted to the handsome Adam as well.

# DANGEROUS WATERS

## Sheila Daglish

On holiday in the enchanting Hungarian village of Szentendre, schoolteacher Cassandra Sutherland meets handsome local artist Matthias Benedek, and soon both are swept up in a romance as dreamy as the moon on the Danube. But Matt is hiding secrets from Cass, and she is determined never to love another man like her late fiance, whose knack for getting into dangerous situations was the ruin of them both. Can love conquer all once it's time for Cass to return home to London?